Claimed by the Barbarian Warlords
Stolen Planet Book 1
Charmaine Ross

Charmaine Ross

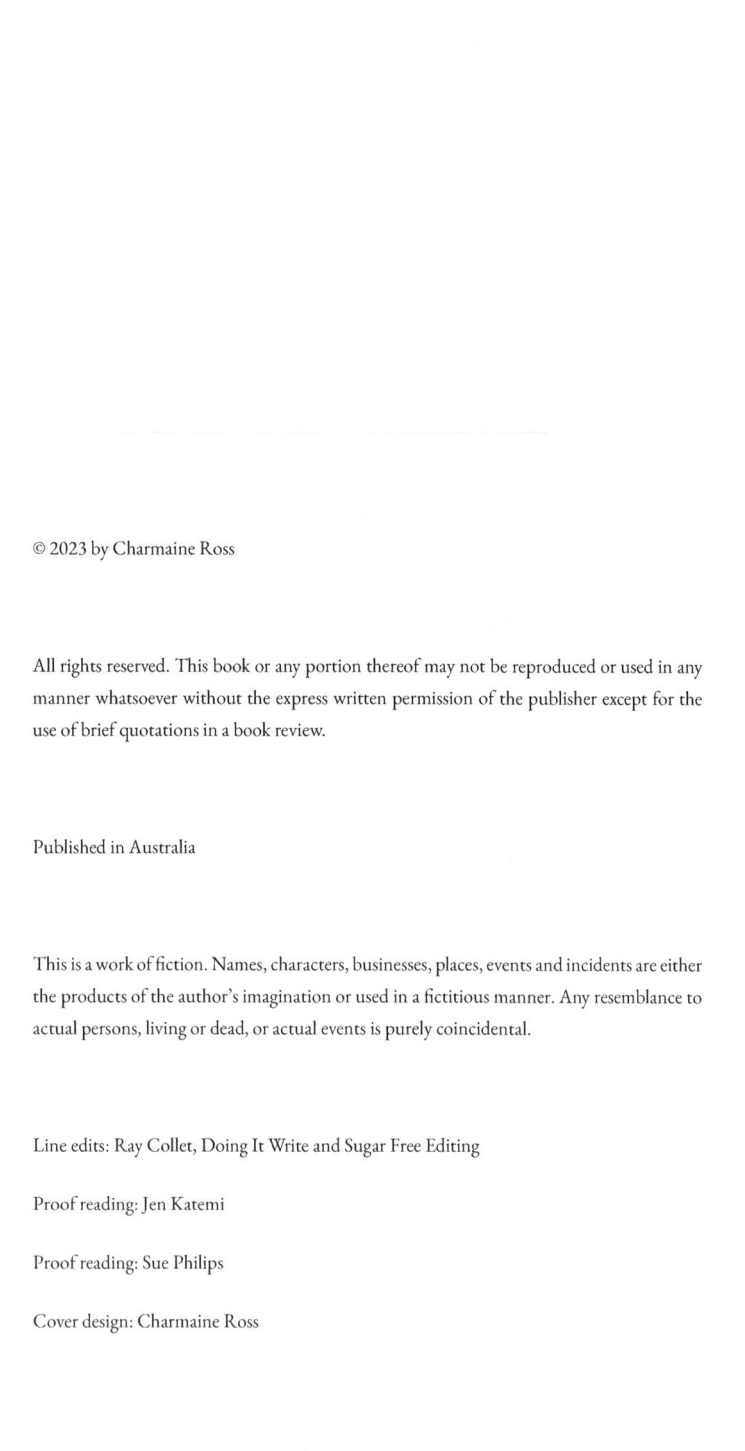

© 2023 by Charmaine Ross

All rights reserved. This book or any portion thereof may not be reproduced or used in any manner whatsoever without the express written permission of the publisher except for the use of brief quotations in a book review.

Published in Australia

This is a work of fiction. Names, characters, businesses, places, events and incidents are either the products of the author's imagination or used in a fictitious manner. Any resemblance to actual persons, living or dead, or actual events is purely coincidental.

Line edits: Ray Collet, Doing It Write and Sugar Free Editing

Proof reading: Jen Katemi

Proof reading: Sue Philips

Cover design: Charmaine Ross

Blurb

Stolen from Earth and captured by alien warlords.

With their crimson skin, pitch-black eyes, and muscles carved from marble, these alphas claim me on the burning fields as their omega mate. I'm not who they think I am, but they're not letting me go, no matter how hard I try to escape.

They tell me I'll enter my heat soon. They tell me I'll beg for their touch, their attentions, their . . . knots. I must resist them before it's too late.

Finding our omega was easy while she's desperate to escape. How can we convince her to stay when she doesn't believe she's ours to pleasure forever?

When I find a rare omega without her protectors, I swoop down to claim her. She says she's human, denies she's our fated mate and fights her biology at every turn.

We'll hold her captive until her heat overcomes her and when she's claimed and bonded, there will be no doubt who she belongs to.

Excerpt

"Not . . . omega . . . human," I manage to strangle out. I want them. No! I want to be back in the safety of my familiar lab. Confusion rolls through me as another surge of heat makes perspiration bead on my forehead.

"Yes, you are, my female. You're all omega." Jet's brows lower and a crease forms between them. "But you're in pain. It will only get worse if your heat isn't eased."

A fog forms inside my head. I understand the words he speaks, but not the meaning. Heat simmers inside my veins, searching for a pinnacle out of my reach. A cramp throbs low in my belly and I groan. I twist and writhe on the bed, wanting something I can't name. "Whatsss heet?"

Stef's brow furrows deeper. "Do you not have omegas where you are from?"

A loud sob escapes me, my body trembling as my pussy throbs uncomfortably. I don't understand what they're talking about. I don't know what's happening to me, but the pain between my legs is growing. My vision wavers as though I'm going to pass out. "N . . . no."

Stef's hand cups my face and I tilt my cheek into his touch. His palm is a soothing balm to the fire erupting inside me. He curses under his breath before turning fathomless eyes on me. "You are an omega. Our perfect half. You're going into heat because we're your alphas. Your body recognizes ours and wants us. This is simple biology. If we don't ease your suffering, it will only get worse."

Their silhouettes blur. I still don't know what he means, but my stomach cramps again, so badly I grunt and curl into a ball. Strong arms lift me from the bed, and I'm cradled on thick thighs. Rif's leather scent wraps around me, and some of the blinding pain magically leeches away.

"My omega. Will you let us touch you and ease your suffering?" Rif's voice sinks through the shimmering pain running through my body. My muscles tense as I tilt on the verge of another cramp. A trickle of sweat runs down my spine and I strain in anticipation of the pain coming my way.

I whine and clutch my stomach, digging fingers into my flesh as if that will hold off the cramp. Stef's fingers trail along my cheek and under my chin. He tilts my head and my eyes flash open. "Look at me, omega. Let us relieve your pain. Please."

His handsome alien face fills my vision, and I hook onto the concern I see on his face. Stef keeps his hand under my chin, while his other hand caresses my thigh. Jet sinks to his knees in front of me, and my thighs part as though I have no ownership of them. Sweet apple blossom drifts around me.

"Hmm, omega. Your scent . . ." His thumb travels over my inner leg, almost to the juncture between them, as his nostrils flare. My clit pulses and wetness weeps from my core. I cry out as my pussy swells with a throbbing need.

The scent of sandalwood makes my mouth water. The mix of cedar and leather is becoming my favorite scent. Pain subsides, giving way to a wave of arousal that soaks through to Rif's muscular thighs. I've never been so wet for a man, let alone three. They aren't men, though. They're demons. Demons turning my insides to liquid desire. My legs fall apart, giving Jet access to my core, yet his hand stays on my thigh. His thumb caresses my jeans-clad legs in circles that drive me wild and make my arousal spiral. Rif's thumb teases the underside of my breasts and Stef's touch whispers along my waist.

I want them to touch me where I ache the most. I need their hands on me. Their fingers inside me. But their hands tease too far away from where I burn for them.

"Use your words, omega. Let us give you the release your body craves. Let us care for you as your alphas should." Rif's voice is low and gravelly. Filled with the same coiled tightness that is strung through me.

I widen my legs and tilt my hips, ready to do anything to take away the burn. I arch my back over the solid support of Rif's arm and thrust my breasts in offer. I don't understand where this level of arousal comes from, but I hurt too much to care. I need this pain to end, need them to touch me, and somehow that makes the most sense of all. My tongue is too thick to say much, so I say the only word I can. "Please."

Contents

1. Chapter One — 1
2. Chapter Two — 9
3. Chapter Three — 18
4. Chapter Four — 30
5. Chapter Five — 40
6. Chapter Six — 52
7. Chapter Seven — 59
8. Chapter Eight — 65
9. Chapter Nine — 74
10. Chapter Ten — 84
11. Chapter Eleven — 96
12. Chapter Twelve — 105
13. Chapter Thirteen — 114
14. Chapter Fourteen — 121
15. Chapter Fifteen — 130
16. Chapter Sixteen — 135
17. Chapter Seventeen — 148
18. Chapter Eighteen — 156

Chapter One

Adele

Before the solar flares hit Earth's atmosphere, I check the lock on my office cabinet and secure my lab equipment. I double-check the data upload to the university's cloud has finished, then download duplicates to my external hard drive before I slip the palm-sized case into my lab coat pocket. One form of backup is never enough to my mind, and who knows if the cloud will even survive the surge of energy that's supposed to hit everyone across the globe.

People went crazy back in two thousand when computer clocks switched over to the new century. Baths were filled with water. Pantries were stocked with food. Everyone made sure they weren't driving in case their cars stopped working, but the clocks ticked over and everything carried on as usual after a collective sigh of relief. These solar flares could be the same, but I guess deep down I'm either a crazy doomsday prepper or a Girl Scout.

Actually, I like to be prepared. I spend far too many hours of my life studying cellular mutation for it to go up in a poof of electronic smoke. My research is too precious. More than precious.

It's my entire life.

I've spent months watching cells divide, thrive, or die beneath my microscope. Some days—most days—pass without me seeing daylight while I'm in the lab. It doesn't matter. What I do here is too important to worry about the cycle of the sun and moon. This is the type of research that could be Earth changing. It would certainly be career changing. I've already garnered interest from Genetech, who wants to be the first company with a cure for all forms of cancer.

I'm a talented scientist, but also a lucky one. I stumbled into a process involving germline mutations of the p53 gene during my undergrad. Patients who carry p53 mutations are rare, but they're at a higher risk of developing many cancers. In particular, oncogenes, which can turn a healthy cell into a cancerous cell. The HER2 is a bastard protein that controls cancer growth and spread. My research stops that protein in its tracks. If my research is successful, I can effectively halve cancer deaths across the world, so if I back up my research on a hundred different devices, it will be worth it.

The p53 gene robbed me of my mother when I was ten and my father just after I turned nineteen. It also left me with a ticking cancer-bomb coded into my body's genetic makeup. Chances are, when I reach a certain age, my cells will start to mutate, and I refuse to be another statistic. To say I'm emotionally invested in this research is an understatement. I've sacrificed my friends, my hours, and my life for it, and I'll be damned if a solar flare will strip it away from me.

The other doctorate students should have made sure everything was off before they left the lab, but they'd been too concerned about getting to the university's solar-flare-inspired "end-of-days" party, which is just an excuse for a gigantic piss up. No one asked if I was going to the party. Not that they'd miss me when I didn't show. I want an early start in the morning, as I've planned to run a test on a new batch of rat cells. I slightly tweaked an active agent I'd manufactured today and am keen for the results. I don't want to waste my time struggling with a hangover.

I flip off another computer, making sure it powers down properly. Luckily, I came back here after dinner. It gave me time to run some particular diagnostics I wanted to get done before tomorrow. Now it's close to midnight, and time to head to my dorm for a few hours of sleep before I return here prior to dawn breaking.

As I reach for the remote to switch off the TV running quietly in the background, my attention snags on the close-up images of the raging sun. The red banner running across the bottom of the screen flashes the word "alert."

A glowing dot forms on the underbelly of the sun. Rapid chatter pours from the TV anchor about how large the sunspot is, and how much damage might occur if it gets too big. They've discussed everything from sunburn to radioactive destruction. I hadn't paid the talk much attention, but as I watch the vision, flames grow larger and higher and the TV anchor quiets as he watches in real time. Strips of burning ropes drift from the sun's surface. The end of one rope skims across the dark of space toward Earth with unanticipated precision.

The television flickers and goes out, leaving static burning the screen. I look out the window to see the night sky glowing red.

The lab's lights go out and the lab equipment is limned in red. Red lightning skitters across the equipment and jumps onto my hand, races up my arm, and sinks into my skin. Energy buzzes through my bones and pulses inside my chest. My heart races and heat infuses my skin. I sway, lightheaded, as though my blood is draining from my body, leaving only my muscles and bones behind.

My feet lift and I rise from the floor, suspended by nothing but air. A pinprick of white light erupts above my head and flashes over me. My body tears apart and I hurtle through a tunnel of light, twisting this way and that. Light streaks past me, or maybe I streak through it. All I know is I'm going at a dizzying pace.

I try to scream, but no sound wrenches from me. There is only blinding light and terror and confusion, going on and on and on. I don't know if I'm even breathing or if my heart is beating.

My body is heavy and light at the same time. I'm being ripped apart cell by cell. The building blocks of my body stack back the right way instead of the haphazard patterns in which they were for the twenty-three years I've been alive. Disharmonious notes inside me blend into a rich chorus.

The light abruptly ends and I'm thrown from the tunnel, my body slamming onto hard-packed dirt. My bones crunch as I roll over several times before I come to a stop. All I can do is lie on the ground, claw the dirt, and cough and gasp and pant, my mind frozen and face streaked with tears and snot.

The white dots dancing in my vision clear, and I'm able to see my surroundings. I almost wish I was blinded by them again. I'm lying among tall strands of wheat, but the strands are midnight black instead of washed-out yellow. They sway, the tips rustle-clattering as they move. There's no wind to make them move. The air is stagnant and heavy with surging humid heat that clings to my body.

The sky above reminds me of burned skin. Red and yellow splotches are bruised with inky black clouds. Blackened smoky particles drift in a heat haze. I inhale and cough when soot fills my lungs. It's then I notice the sound of flames. Not the friendly crackle of flickering flames in a campfire, but the roar of an out-of-control fire. The type of fire that wipes out houses and forests and burns people alive when they're taken by surprise and left with no time to run.

I come up on my elbow, peeking over the black wheat, and see a wall of flame bearing down on me, so hot the air vibrates and shimmers. I scramble to my feet and stumble, legs buckling. I sprawl onto the ground, landing atop the wheat, sharp tips cutting through my lab coat and my skin. Blood blooms, liquid red over the white fabric, but thankfully I'm in no pain. I'm too out-of-my-mind scared to be anything but fear personified.

I glance over my shoulder to see the fire bearing toward me impossibly fast. I scramble to my feet and run through the sea of black blades. My throat is dry and my lungs burn as I try to outrun the fire even though I have no chance. Survival instincts are strange like that.

A roar booms around me and the ground shakes. Water explodes to my right and shoots into the air as though a dam has broken, only it streaks into the sky instead of pouring into a catchment basin, shooting higher and higher until it reaches its zenith and rains scalding hot water down on me.

I fall to my knees and hunch over. I bring my lab coat over my head, crying out in agony as my collarbone grates, but then I don't think about my bones as water pounds onto my back and forces me to the ground beneath its weight. It turns the dirt into instant mud, and I gasp for air when muck fills my mouth. I'm under a waterfall. A terrible, scalding-hot, never-ending waterfall that scorches my skin and clogs my lungs.

The water keeps falling and I think I'm going to pass out, but then the force of it weakens. Splattering drops rain down and stop. I'm bruised all over, my limbs so weak I can barely move. The ground quakes and I know another water geyser is going to erupt, maybe this time right below me.

I somehow get my legs under me and stagger upright. The water has put out the raging fire, but steam rises in thick blankets. I breathe in cloying humidity, coughing, eyes streaming. I don't think I can take another step. Maybe this is it for me. Maybe I die before cancer has had a chance to mutate and ravage my body—before I've had a chance to cure the millions.

An alarmed shout snags my attention. Blurry figures run toward me, slashing through the black wheat. I swipe the tears from my eyes. My heart stops racing before it punches my chest in a pounding beat, and my mind tries to find reason where there is none to be found. These figures, at least twenty of them, are not people. These are creatures with red skin. Black horns spiral from their temples and rise over their skulls. Thick black hair falls across their shoulders and halfway down their backs. They are not human. They're not even from mythology. They are terrifying, otherworldly beasts that make my brain stutter and halt. I must have died and my soul is in hell because these demons straight out of hell are descending on me.

They charge toward me on powerful, thick legs. Draped over their hips and thighs are black loin cloths made from flimsy leather strips. Their high-waisted skirts only accentuate their toned torsos—pecs formed from solid, defined muscle and broad shoulders that are four times as wide as mine. Their biceps bulge as they slash through the wheat with sweeping, powerful strokes from long, silver swords.

They have no eyes. Just a broad blackened strip across their faces that goes from temple to temple. Thick white canines drop onto their bottom lips. They're running at me, and I'm clearly their sole focus.

A gust of wind rakes steam across the ground and obscures them from me. I force my legs to work and stumble away from the demons. I ignore the stalks that cut through my jeans and stain the denim red with my blood. A few gashes will be nothing if these creatures catch me.

The steam swallows me. I surge forward, but a figure lunges through the haze. His powerful arms stretch as he swipes black, claw-tipped fingers toward me. He is a whole head and shoulders taller than me. I scream, turn on my heel, and bolt away from him. The steam drifts on the breeze and clears, allowing me to see the creatures

I'm running toward. I stagger to a stop, then turn in a circle to find them surrounding me and closing in.

I sob out loud, unable to contain the blinding terror that rips through me. My body shakes. My knees wobble, but I refuse to go down without a fight. I'll struggle as hard as I can. I'll kick and claw, scratch and bite.

They converge around me, caging me in a contracting formation. This close I realize they do have eyes, but the sclera, iris, and pupils are a flat, gleaming black and indistinguishable with the horizontal patch of black paint across their upper faces. Made from the dregs of my nightmares, they are chilling creatures. I must be dead. There's no other reason to witness these beings. The tunnel stole me from my lab and threw me into hell. My muscles turn to liquid and I wonder what I did to deserve an eternity of torture because if there's one thing I'm sure of, it's that there is no place on Earth like this.

I clench my fists, draw together as much courage as I possess, and yell, "Don't come any closer!"

They stop stalking me and mutter to each other. I hear growls and voices so low they are just rumbly sounds. The looks I get are slightly confused, but one of them lifts his head, closes his eyes. His nostrils flare as he drags in air. His tongue flickers from his mouth like a snake.

His barrel-sized head lowers and he pins me with a look that pulses through me. "Awmygha."

The word is absolute and cements itself within me. The air charges with something far more terrible than fire and smoke and scalding hot water as feral looks pass between the demons. My insides pulse and the place between my legs throbs, like a physical touch. I look down to see what might have stroked me, but there's nothing.

A snarl rips from one creature's lips, and they charge toward me as though I'm some sort of prize. Panic takes control, but there is nowhere I can run. I'm surrounded and I know when they reach me, I will not survive what they have in store for me. I run anyway because my mind and body demand I fight, no matter how the odds stack against me.

A whooshing sound beats above my head. Wind whips my hair and clothes, and a roar louder than any made by the demons vibrates through me. I look up, the breath catching in my lungs, to see a demon riding a great winged horse streaking toward me. Its flaming mane of red, orange, and yellow accentuates its thick black armor and gleaming midnight coat. Its wings are as wide as a bus, its sleek flack feathers tipped by burning reds and yellows.

The demon riding the horse is the most horrifying. He's massive. Bigger than the other demons by another half a head at least. Long black hair streams behind him. His eyes are narrowed, his lips peeled back, revealing fangs big enough to rip my throat open with one simple tear. He is terrifying in his stunning, masculine beauty.

His arm stretches out as the horse swoops. He holds the reins in one hand, his thick fingers wrapping around the black chain with expert ease. Self-preservation kicks in and I turn and run, but I'm too slow. His arm bands around my middle. His muscles are solid, his grip sure as he plucks me off the ground. I'm swept into the air and crushed against his massive chest that smells of smoky leather and sin.

I thrash, but his steel muscles don't let me go. He traps me against his body so I can barely move. He is simply too big and powerful.

His low growl sounds in my ear, and a wash of heated air spills across the side of my face from his fiery breath. I'm too scared to move. I'm a ragged, panting mess—a rabbit trapped between a wolf's jaws, waiting for them to close around my neck and end my life, and there's nothing I can do.

Chapter Two

Rhifgraugdk

The female is an *omega*. I tip back my head and roar my triumph, my blood pumping like liquid fire through my veins. She trembles. Her heart pounds in her chest and her breaths are shallow little pants. The acidic scent of fear wafts from her pores and stings my nose. She is terrified, my little omega, but in my arms she will know nothing but safety and comfort, although she may not understand that yet.

She is the most precious being in all the universes to me. If she knew this, her teeth wouldn't clack in fear. She would know I just saved her from a rutting pack of alphas who lost control when they scented her. I am stronger than they are and don't lose control. I'm their warlord and a great alpha. They bend to me in all things, as will this little omega. I can almost taste her submission on my tongue.

She wears strange clothing; a white coat that is too big for her small frame twists around her body, and underneath I spy a knitted pink top and tight leg coverings made from a thick navy-blue material. Black boots cover her feet. I wish to rip her clothing off her fragile body and see what she's like underneath. She is nothing like an Amadonian.

She lacks the horns, tail, fangs, and tough skin of our kind. A curious creature that is all warm female, nonetheless. Rare. Precious.

Omega.

My salvation and that of my bond brothers.

An unprotected omega at that. I do not know how she came to be in the burning fields or how long she had been there. The cleansing fires are no place for any female when the fields burn at the change of season. It was only because I was patrolling and overseeing the hardiest of my alphas that I saw her running from them.

Blackened land streaks beneath me as I urge Torbjorn to fly as fast as he can, spotting none of her protectors. Who in their right minds would let a precious omega run free? My hand itches to draw my broadsword and sever their heads for this travesty.

Year in, year out, there have been fewer omegas born, and we have found none for ten years. Those of breeding age are entering middle age now. Without omegas, there will be no alphas or omegas born, leaving only a population of betas. Our planet will lose its last line of protection in our alpha army because betas are weak and easily controlled. Our planet, once a thriving metropolis, has been reduced to six warring sectors, with a few thousand people in each. The Ulgix have been working on a cure for our people since the decline in omegas was first noticed, but it has dropped off too fast in these last few decades.

I turn my attention to this omega. This peculiar female. Our omega. Our salvation. I will be forever thankful for however she came to be here. That is a mystery for another day. Now I will satisfy my alpha instincts and hers, claim her and breed her, as is an alpha's right to the omega he finds.

"Min ayn aint alsaghir," I say. *Where are you from, little one*? She doesn't answer. She whimpers, half out of her head with distress. Her scent doesn't lie. She is petrified. My stomach twists with the strident scent. She should only know safety in the arms of her alphas.

"Kayf jit litakun fi harayiq altathir?" *How did you come to be in the cleansing fires?* She doesn't answer. Her breath shivers in and out between her pink lips and she holds herself still, or as still as her shaking form allows.

"Hal tafhamunaa?" *Do you understand me?* Her breath hitches and shakes as much as her body. She remains unresponsive, and now I determine she must not understand my language.

I scent blood. Red oozes through the tears in her clothing, and I kick myself for being so oblivious to her wounds. Her clothing is streaked with it. Her blood. She must have been cut by the razor-sharp heads of the aefedoss and another reason I would see her protectors die. A creature so soft should be nowhere near the stalks when the regenerating fires raze the land. Her pain slices through me as if it were my own.

Already I sense our *aitisal alruwh* as my soul reaches out for hers, finding a whirlwind of confusion and anguish. I can't penetrate that buzzing, dark cloud. Not yet. Not until she is ready to accept my bond brothers and myself, and fuse our souls forever. I swallow my disappointment. I want to crush her to me, to show her I won't harm a bone in her body. I tilt back her head, wrapping my hand around her neck to settle her. Her eyes lose focus and her mouth opens, slack.

My breath catches in my lungs at the color of her eyes. Ice-blue and white. A ring of light-blue around the swollen black in its center. Her eyes are nothing like the total black of ours, which protects us from the constant fires of the land.

Everything about her is soft and helpless. She is softer than an Amadonian female. Much softer. She has a high, smooth forehead, and sleek brows the same color as her pure, flowing hair. Her nose is straight, turning up at its tip, but her lips capture my full attention. Pink and plump. I've never seen such a beautiful, exotic creature in my life. My cock swells as I imagine those lips wrapped around my shaft. Soon they will be. When she enters her famed omega heat, I will offer all parts of myself to soothe her through it.

Her heat will trigger my alpha rut. It's a pleasure I've never had, and one I thought I would never experience. It will be my duty and honor to see her through it, and also something my bond brothers and I will very much enjoy.

With her in my arms, it is only a matter of time before my pheromones trigger her heat. With the three of us, she will willingly offer her neck and her soul to us. I will not think twice when I sink my teeth into her and bond her to me, as will Stefnan and Jaetvard. Already her scent is beginning to change with my alpha presence, slipping her into heat, but before it takes over her body, I'll make sure her injuries are treated and a translator implanted to reduce her fear.

She says something and rakes my forearm, trying to dig her blunt claws into my skin, but there's no way they will penetrate my tough hide. I offer her a smile to calm her. Her gaze catches on my fangs and a shiver works through her whole body.

Her voice is soft and sweet, her language lilting and seductive. Everything about this omega has me captivated. Omegas are naturally submissive. They detect their alphas' moods and become attuned to them, seeking their approval, the two working in tandem, or so my mother told me before The Death took her from me. My fathers soon followed their love into the after-fires, and within three months I'd lost all my parents.

My omega thrashes in my arms, kicking her legs and trying to scratch my arm. There is no way she can hurt me, but Torbjorn whinnies, disturbed that I might be hurting her. Her booted heel thumps against my thigh. I barely feel it, although I know she's put as much strength into it as she can.

"Qif. Sawf tudhi nafsak." *Stop. You will hurt yourself,* I say in my most soothing tone. It's not one I have mastered, thanks to our lack of omegas. Nor my bond brothers. As warlords, we have little need to soothe anyone. Instead we expect them to bow to us as the most feared and powerful alphas in our kingdom.

The omega sinks her blunt white teeth into my arm. Her jaw compresses and she growls. Her bite does nothing more than pinch my skin, but her growl goes straight to my cock, which hardens immediately.

She knows what's pressing against her backside when her eyes flare open and understanding floods their pure depths. There's no way she can mistake the size and girth of an alpha's cock. I imagine how round her curious eyes will grow when I work my knot into her sweet pussy. How the smooth wet glide of her will feel around my length. Now a growl passes from the depths of *my* chest.

Her teeth slide free of my skin. She gasps. There is a moment of stillness just before she lashes at me in pure panic. She curls her little hands into fists and pummels them against my solid chest. Omegas are meant to be submissive, but I like her fire. I like the way she gives in to her rage and tries her best to protect herself. This is no weak omega. This is an omega worthy of an alpha of my strength and power. I have indeed found a prize. The protectors who lost her are fools.

Her fists strike my jaw, my shoulder, anywhere she can land a punch. Her strikes are nothing more than taps, but her legs flail and her heel accidentally strikes Torbjorn before I can subdue her.

The savimite whinnies and loses a beat of his massive wings. We plummet toward the ground, his colorful, flaming feathers, made from light and fire, streaming around us. I'm used to riding my stallion, but my omega isn't. She screams. The sound she makes is high and shrill and cuts straight to my heart. Her heart stutters as pure alarm shoots through her. I need to calm her before she has a heart attack, so I do the only thing I can think of that ensures the control of an omega.

I lock my thighs around Torbjorn's muscular shoulders so we won't fall from the saddle, then I lean down and collect her lips in mine. They're plump and soft and I groan as her taste seeps into my mouth. Pure ambrosia. Nothing will taste better, except perhaps when I lick her cunt, feast on her slick, and bury myself in her heat.

I can't stop myself from kissing her now that I have her taste. I sweep my tongue into her honeyed depths. Never before had I realized what I missed. I eat her lips, drawing her tongue into my mouth and sucking before releasing it. I lick her plump bottom lip, digging my fangs into the tender strip of flesh, only lightly enough not to prick her. Just enough to tell her who will master her body and bring her unbelievable pleasure.

She kisses me back, her scent wrapping around us both as her arousal grows. I do this to her. I make this omega slick with desire. Satisfaction rears through me, knowing I've taken her fight away. Her lips loosen and she sags in my arms. Triumph roars through my blood when she sucks my bottom lip into her hot wetness, then pain streaks through me when she bites down hard enough to draw blood.

I reel back and wipe my lip with the back of my hand, staring at the smudge of crimson blood on my crimson skin. My little omega is a warrior! My blood sings with exultant glory as lust shoots through me and spears straight through to my cock. It throbs behind my battle leathers, and my knot pulses in readiness. I need this omega. I am ready to rut her for days, lock her body to mine so there will be no misunderstanding who she belongs to. Heat bursts over me as I imagine being joined with her, shooting my cum into her willing body time after time.

"'Ant li ya litil 'uwmigha." *You are mine, little omega.* As the words are a promise of what is to come, electric lightning shoots over my body as it prepares for rut. It jumps from my skin onto hers. She stiffens, her mouth falling open, a strangled cry erupting from her lips. Her eyes roll back into their sockets before she goes limp.

There is something terribly wrong. Her white coat seeps with more of her red blood. I notice her arm is folded across her chest and that one of her shoulders bulges at an unnatural angle. I curse myself. She is more injured than I thought. Only her sense of self-preservation allowed her to fight me until her body gave out.

I kick Torbjorn's sides, urging him to fly swifter. "Faster, my friend. Hurry!"

My heart hammers as I hold the omega, who is now too still in my arms. Her head lolls backward as it flops over my arm. She's in bad shape. Anger flashes through me as I wonder who would have done something like this to such a delicate creature, but until I can get her healed and speak to her, I will have to bide my time until I seek vengeance.

I urge Torbjorn to fly so low his wings brush the tops of the outer farm dwellings of my land. Finally, my castle approaches. We skim over the defensive wall made from solid Fyette wood, hard enough to last centuries once dried and treated correctly from the cleansing fires hot enough to turn wood into stone. The poles stand erect, sharpened into points, protecting the township inside.

My people look up as I fly overhead, capturing their attention. From blacksmiths pounding armor, to tanners drying skins, and females trading cakes and watching kits run and tumble beneath their feet.

I pull Torbjorn's reins and we shoot upward to the topmost tower that houses the suites I share with my bond brothers. Wind tears at my hair and clothing, we fly so fast.

"Stefnan!" I call. My booming voice carries far and after a moment, Stefnan steps onto my balcony. He blinks, as though making sure he's correctly seeing the precious bundle I carry before his mouth falls open. My second is a battle-hardened warrior like myself, but at the sight of an omega, his demeanor changes instantly.

His nostrils flare and horror passes over his features when he sees the poor state of the female in my arms. "You have an omega?"

Torbjorn's hooves clatter on the stone as I guide him to land on my balcony. He thrashes his head and stomps his six hooves, making a racket. His flesh twitches and his mouth foams with exertion. He has pushed himself to protect my omega.

I'm off Torbjorn in an instant, stalking through my open door. "Send for D'Kali. Quickly!"

Stefnan takes a staggering step toward us. "She's injured!"

I lay my precious omega on my bed, worried she hasn't moved for too long. Standing back, I see how much damage her body has taken.

I wheel around to Stef, cutting through his shock. "I fear she's gravely hurt. We need D'Kali urgently."

Stef cups her cheek with his massive palm, his claws carefully retracted before he dares touch her. Already he is lost to her as much as I am. "Whoever did this to her will pay with their lives after I rip their intestines out and roast them in the flames."

Jaetvard will feel the same when he sees her. We will hunt her protectors and raze them to the ground, just like the healing fires. They lost their right to live when she received the first cut to her skin.

"You will tell me everything when I return," he says.

I nod, and he bolts out of the room without further questions, leaving me with my unconscious female. I will do anything to ensure she lives. I will do anything for my precious omega.

Chapter Three

Adele

When I wake, I don't drift up through gray layers of dreamy fluff like in the movies. I scream out of unconsciousness, thrust upward by the hard slap of agony. I'm nothing but one big throbbing mass of bone and muscle. Every breath inflates my lungs with razor blades. I thrash in an attempt to outrun the pain, but large, firm hands hold me down on a soft surface.

A low growl vibrates through me. My body goes limp, the sound traveling through me and slaking my panic, although I don't know why. I have good reason to be terrified.

I recognize that sound. My watery eyes focus on the demon with his large hands on my shoulders. My vision clears to see that his face is close to mine. He has human-like features—eyes, nose, mouth—but they are strange and different. His straight brows are slashes over solid black eyes. His nose is angular and straight and set above wide, well-formed lips. His cheeks are chiseled slabs of flesh that drop to a cutting jawline. Then there are the dual thick, black horns spiraling from his temples, framing the sides of his skull. The tips are sharp enough to gut me with the flick of his head if he wishes. He is handsome and terrifying all at once.

He says something to me tinged with a deep growl, and his fangs peek from the corners of his mouth. His sharp, shiny, white fangs. I fill my lungs and scream despite the pain it brings to my body. I try to roll away, but he is stronger and pins me down too easily.

He turns his head and speaks. Movement at the corner of my eye catches my attention. Another face leans close to me, but this face is horrifying and terrifyingly alien.

Reptilian.

This being is something crossed between a lizard and a snake. Yellow eyes stare down at me from a large, bulbous head, eyes wide with shock, then something dark and calculating shifts in his gaze as he studies me. His nose is flat. He has no lips, just a broad slit for a mouth. His face is green and instead of hair, splotches of darker green cover his bald head.

His head swivels on a thick neck, and his voice is a mess of hisses and slithery sounds. I thrash against the demon holding me down, kicking and scratching as though my life depends on it. Maybe it does. I don't care about the burning agony lashing through my body. It's secondary when compared to getting away from the monster.

The demon barks a command. He leans on me, trapping my arms and legs with his much bigger body, and presses me into the mattress. A large hand covers my cheek and turns my head to bare my neck. No matter how hard I struggle, I can't move against his sheer weight and power.

He holds me still as the reptile beast presses something to my biceps. I feel a pinch and my body fills with liquid tranquility. All the aches and pains disappear. My arms drop beside me and I relax, uncaring that the demon and the monster still hover above me.

My bones are limp noodles. My muscles are inconsequential. I float just out of reach of the terror that gripped me, and I don't care. Nothing can touch me in the space I'm in. The demon snarls something else at him. The reptile brings a silver gun and places it behind my ear. He presses a trigger. A thump echoes through my head, but thankfully, there's no pain. Just an echo that goes through the hollow mush inside my head.

The demon collects my cheek in his palm and turns my head so that he can look down at me. "Can you understand me now, little omega?"

My mouth falls open. "U speek Engleesh nuw?" My tongue is dead in my mouth and won't form words properly.

The demon's straight brows drop low over his charcoal eyes. "You gave her too much serum!" His booming voice blooms through me, tinted with agitation and anger, and I let the tone sink into my bones as though they are soft bubbles.

My eyes drift across the demon's crimson skin. My fingers twitch with the urge to run over all those delicious, bulging arm muscles before I frown. I shouldn't want to do that, but for the life of me I can't think why that is so important.

"I had to estimate the dose. Rest assured, she feels no pain, my lord," the reptile says before gazing at me with glinting yellow eyes. I don't like the way he looks at me, as though I'm not a person, but a thing. The look vanishes when the demon turns to him.

"Icn un'stan uuutoooo," I say. Funny, when I can also hear the reptile's clicks and hisses in the background. "I haaav too voicssss inmy hed."

I should be terrified that my brain has stopped working properly. Nothing makes sense. These creatures shouldn't exist and I shouldn't be able to understand them so clearly. Not unless I died in the solar flare and I'm in the underworld. It would explain why a demon is looking at me as though he wants to eat me alive. Still, I don't panic the way I think I should. My body and my brain are numb. Deliciously numb.

The demon turns back to me, his eyes, dark as coal, raking over my body. His body heat infuses with my skin through the palm cupping my cheek. My nostrils flare with the scent of leather. I turn my head into his palm and sniff. The scent washes off his skin and fills my lungs.

My mind and body might be numb, but my stomach tightens strangely. A dull cramp pulls deep within the cradle of my hips before releasing, and a corresponding throb explodes between my legs. Wetness trickles between my thighs, and a sweet apple-blossom scent rises around me.

A frown tightens my brow. "Doooo uuuu have flooowersss?" Talking is far too hard with the size of my tongue. The muscle fills my mouth and sticks to the top in dryness.

Movement over the demon's shoulder catches my attention. Another demon stands behind the one who stole me on that horse made of fire. He is as big and imposing as the demon holding me as though I might break. Where he has pitch-black hair, this new demon has electric-blue hair that flows over his shoulders and halfway down his back. His hair is braided into thick strands, with golden beads woven throughout.

"How is the omega?" The other demon takes a step toward me, and my demon's lips pull back. A snarl sounds from his lips, deep and intimidating. His body swells, growing bigger and more muscular in an instant. His chest bulges with delicious dips and ridges, and his biceps are thicker than my thighs. It makes the blue-haired demon step back at the same time as a languid heat rolls through me.

"Calm, Rif. I'll not hurt her. She is precious to me too," the demon says.

So Rif is the demon who smells like sin and leather. His shoulders drop but he twitches, like he has tamed a beast inside him. "Apologies, Stef. I find it hard to control my urges."

Stef's eyes fill with awe and fire as he approaches me slowly, as though he can't quite believe what he's looking at. My nostrils flare as cedar mingles with leather. "That's understandable, brother. Tell me where you found her."

Rif looks down at me, and I tumble into his dark eyes. "She was in the cleansing fires without her protectors."

Stef growls and his eyes flash. My stomach pulls in that sweet way that makes me feel hot and floaty.

"And an omega who looks like . . . *her*. Alone?" Another demon stomps through the door to stand next to Stef. His gaze rakes my body from the top of my head to my toes as though he's stripping me down and building me into something new. Something I can't name. This demon's hair is silvery-white and falls like a shower of silk over his broad shoulders. Sandalwood mingles with cedar and leather, and the scent makes my mouth water.

I flinch at the tremor of wariness that sinks into me at being surrounded by so much muscle. The air practically vibrates with testosterone. Or maybe that's just coming from the massive demon tucked into my side.

"It's all right, omega. They are my bond brothers, Stef and Jaetvard—Jet. Your mates now. They'll never harm you," Rif says, gesturing at one behemoth, then the other.

I don't trust a word he says because the two demons he points to look at me as though they do want to harm me. I'm sure they want to take a bite out of me and chew me up. It definitely doesn't make me feel any safer.

I don't understand what omega means. Or what bond brothers are. But my cares slip through my mind like oil. Instead I wonder what their skin would feel like against mine. It looks velvety, almost like suede. I lift my heavy hand, curving my fingers around Rif's thick biceps. He's warm. Almost too hot, but his body heat sinks through my skin, sending tingles straight between my thighs. Wetness seeps from my core again, soaking my underwear as desire spirals through me, heady with its strength. I work saliva into my mouth as I shift on the bed. "Rif?"

His nostrils flare as another cloud of apple blossom wafts around us. "I love my name on your lips, omega. My full name is Rhifgraugdk Thorvaldsson. Stefnan, Jaetvard, and I are the prime warlords of the Rjúkaland, and we rule over all souls who live here."

Rif smiles at me—a predator's smile mixed with heat and tenderness and white-hot possession all rolled into one simple lift of that luscious mouth. His canines peek between his plump lips that are a darker crimson than that of his skin. I fall into that smile, tumbling head over heels down an endless tunnel even as I realize that he has beautiful lips. Plump lips I want to kiss and flick my tongue across and sweep my tongue through to taste his hot, wet mouth and ... what the hell is wrong with me?

Flames flick underneath my skin and I draw in a shaky breath, wondering where these thoughts are coming from. These *needs*. The air is tinted with leather, cedar, and sandalwood scents that obscure all else. They fill my lungs, and my heart thumps like a hammer against an anvil, making me forget I never responded like this to any man. But he isn't a man, is he? He's a demon, and I should be afraid of all of them.

My body didn't get the memo. Heat rises through me. My core clenches as desire rages between my thighs. I think I might have soiled myself, but Rif takes one look at my pelvis, his black eyes flaring wide before uttering, "Leave us, D'Kali."

"But . . . Sire . . . If I can just get a sample of her blood," the green lizard, D'Kali, says. He waves his claw-tipped fingers as though he doesn't want to leave his latest experiment. I understand that look, because it's the same way I look at a batch of cells under my microscope when I know I'm onto something that may change the course of human history.

The reptile wants me on a petri dish because I am something for him to dissect. Something to poke and prod. A body without a mind or feelings or skin that will bleed when cut. An enigma he means to explore, no matter the cost.

"A sample? Why?" Stef asks, his brows drawing low. Something clenches in me at the rough tone of his voice. If I ever heard a warning, that was it, but the reptile seems oblivious.

The lizard monster gestures to my prone form. "I can make sure she doesn't get sick. She's an omega. You can't risk *The Death* getting to her . . ."

"No!" I whisper. *The Death*? I draw in a sharp breath, shrinking away from the reptile and into Rif as much as my heavy body can move, my skin crawling as D'Kali's oily gaze rakes over me. I don't want that being coming anywhere near me. The demons are predators, but the reptile will tear me apart without a second thought. I don't know where I am or how I even came to be here, but the remaining part of my mind understands that.

Jet roars and strides to D'Kali, towering over him as he grows in bulk. "Get out!" His voice shakes the bed beneath me.

"It's not wise to come between alphas and their omega," Stef says, caging D'Kali in on his other side.

D'Kali hovers for a moment, and when his yellow eyes narrow on me before he turns away, I know I'm a target. He slinks from the room, shuts the door behind him, and I'm the sole focus of three pairs of intense eyes. My pussy clenches. Lust rears over me, washing through my body with a wave of intense heat.

"Wha . . ." I try to speak, but my mind is nothing more than molasses. Whatever D'Kali did to me has sunk deep into my bones. I sway between intense arousal and lying in a puddle of my own liquefied bones.

Stef sinks to his knees next to Rif, touching my cheek, my arm, my thigh. His hand keeps moving as though he can't decide where to rest it. Or perhaps he wants to touch me all over at once and one part of me is not enough.

Jet moves to my other side and they cage me in like they did D'Kali, but the difference is that my body is on fire beneath their intensity, while D'Kali had been enraged.

Jet reaches for me. His hand shakes, hovering over me as though he can't believe I'm real.

"Watch your claws, Jet. She's fragile," Rif barks.

Jet hisses and the long black claws at the end of his fingers retract before he clenches his fist and pulls away. Goosebumps skate over my skin as sudden throbbing pain blooms through me. I groan, my own hands shaking as I flatten them over my stomach.

"She needs your touch too, Jet. Touch her and ease her pain, brother," Rif growls.

Jet swallows. He reaches toward me again, tentative, but as he draws close, the throb inside me eases. I sigh when his hand skims along my waist with a light touch. "I don't know how you came to be in the cleansing fires, but I vow to kill whoever was so careless with one as precious as you."

"Not precious." I gasp.

A growl rumbles from his chest, making me suck in a quick breath because. *That. Sound.*

"Omega, you are precious beyond comprehension." He skims his fingers over my waist, just below my breasts, making my nipples bead into diamond hard points. I thrust my breasts upward as though something needy inside me has taken over.

The ache gets worse as Rif drops his palm to my thigh and Stef curves his large hand over my hip. There's no reason why I should burn for their touch, but I do. The possessive way they hold me makes my insides glow. All I can think about is wanting them to touch me where I need it the most.

"How?" I choke out, needing to force myself to think of something else rather than their unbearably delicious touches.

I shouldn't want to be touched by demons. It should repulse me, but the opposite is true. It's against my better judgment, but I'm drawn to them all in a way I've never experienced before. It doesn't make any sense, but even knowing that doesn't stop the arousal skating through me.

Rif's eyes settle on me and his hand curves about the opposite hip held by Stef. Long, black, lethal claws dimple my clothing before he retracts them into his fingertips. "You're going into heat because your body recognizes your alphas. We'll be driven to rut too if you keep smelling so tempting, but you're in no condition to sheath our cocks. Not just yet. Not the way in which we'll need to take you to make you ours."

The molasses in my mind stutters to a stop as a frisson of heat bubbles through me. His words act as though they are drugs, sinking into me and making heat rear through my body. My mouth waters as his fingers continue to brush over my skin, each stroke more hypnotizing than the last.

"Not...omega...human," I manage to strangle out. I want them. No! I want to be back in the safety of my familiar lab. Confusion rolls through me as another surge of heat makes perspiration bead on my forehead.

"Yes, you are, my female. You're all omega." Jet's brows lower and a crease forms between them. "But you're in pain. It will only get worse if your heat isn't eased."

A fog forms inside my head. I understand the words he speaks, but not the meaning. Heat simmers inside my veins, searching for a pinnacle out of my reach. A cramp throbs low in my belly and I groan. I twist and writhe on the bed, wanting something I can't name. "Whatsss heet?"

Stef's brow furrows deeper. "Do you not have omegas where you are from?"

A loud sob escapes me, my body trembling as my pussy throbs uncomfortably. I don't understand what they're talking about. I don't know what's happening to me, but the pain between my legs is growing. My vision wavers as though I'm going to pass out. "N . . . no."

Stef's hand cups my face and I tilt my cheek into his touch. His palm is a soothing balm to the fire erupting inside me. He curses under his breath before turning fathomless eyes on me. "You are an omega. Our perfect half. You're going into heat because we're your alphas. Your body recognizes ours and wants us. This is simple biology. If we don't ease your suffering, it will only get worse."

Their silhouettes blur. I still don't know what he means, but my stomach cramps again, so badly I grunt and curl into a ball. Strong arms lift me from the bed, and I'm cradled on thick thighs.

Rif's leather scent wraps around me, and some of the blinding pain magically leeches away.

"My omega. Will you let us touch you and ease your suffering?" Rif's voice sinks through the shimmering pain running through my body. My muscles tense as I tilt on the verge of another cramp. A trickle of sweat runs down my spine and I strain in anticipation of the pain coming my way.

I whine and clutch my stomach, digging fingers into my flesh as if that will hold off the cramp. Stef's fingers trail along my cheek and under my chin. He tilts my head and my eyes flash open. "Look at me, omega. Let us relieve your pain. Please."

His handsome alien face fills my vision, and I hook onto the concern I see on his face. Stef keeps his hand under my chin, while his other hand caresses my thigh. Jet sinks to his knees in front of me, and my thighs part as though I have no ownership of them. Sweet apple blossom drifts around me.

"Hmm, omega. Your scent . . ." His thumb travels over my inner leg, almost to the juncture between them, as his nostrils flare. My clit pulses and wetness weeps from my core. I cry out as my pussy swells with a throbbing need.

The scent of sandalwood makes my mouth water. The mix of cedar and leather is becoming my favorite scent. Pain subsides, giving way to a wave of arousal that soaks through to Rif's muscular thighs. I've never been so wet for a man, let alone three. They aren't men, though. They're demons. Demons turning my insides to liquid desire. My legs fall apart, giving Jet access to my core, yet his hand stays on my thigh. His thumb caresses my jeans-clad legs in circles that drive me wild and make my arousal spiral. Rif's thumb teases the underside of my breasts and Stef's touch whispers along my waist.

I want them to touch me where I ache the most. I need their hands on me. Their fingers inside me. But their hands tease too far away from where I burn for them.

"Use your words, omega. Let us give you the release your body craves. Let us care for you as your alphas should." Rif's voice is low and gravelly. Filled with the same coiled tightness that is strung through me.

I widen my legs and tilt my hips, ready to do anything to take away the burn. I arch my back over the solid support of Rif's arm and thrust my breasts in offer. I don't understand where this level of arousal comes from, but I hurt too much to care. I need this pain to end, need them to touch me, and somehow that makes the most sense of all. My tongue is too thick to say much, so I say the only word I can. "Please."

Chapter Four

Adele

A tremble works through Stef's large frame. A hot breath rushes from Rif's mouth to ruffle my hair and tickle my ear. I shiver, waiting for Jet's hand to cup my core where I weep for him. Instead, his hand drifts to the dip of my waist and skates over my shoulder to wrap around the base of my neck.

"I feel your pulse, omega. It beats like a drum for us. Only us." Rif's voice is a rough growl that melts my insides.

The possession in his words strike a primal chord deep inside me I never knew existed. Then again, I'm not in my right mind. These demons are weaving a seductive web around me, and I'm caught in the middle. A far part of my mind cries out that nothing about my situation is right. That I really shouldn't be so aroused under these circumstances, but Rif's thumb strokes along my jawline and he leans toward me and the thought dissolves in the face of hedonistic want.

"I'm going to kiss you, my omega. I will claim your mouth and then you will find your pleasure with our hands."

Stef cups my nape with a large hand, holding my head steady so that Rif can devour my mouth. His lips capture mine in an instant, and his tongue dives into my mouth, swallowing my moan. His scent is more potent on my tongue. Leather melts into me, liquifying my muscles. His taste is ambrosia, satisfying the insatiable, needy ache twisting inside me. He groans and the vibrations from his voice sink inside me.

"You are ours, omega. Only ours," Stef murmurs before Rif captures my mouth again.

I don't doubt his words. I am theirs. At this moment, I want nothing more than their hands, mouths, teeth, cocks. Need throbs through me, bordering on pain, and if I don't have someone's hand between my thighs right now, I will explode. Driven by an undeniable urge, I shove my hand between my damp thighs to relieve the tight pressure coiling there.

I've never been this wanton, this forward, but another creature has awoken inside me and taken control of my actions, driving me to do unacceptable things that make no sense. I can't stop myself. I want them to touch me. I want their attention. A part of me knows I shouldn't allow them, but the other, larger part is hyper-focused on the salacious need driving me.

"This pleasure is mine to give," Jet growls. His hand skims up my thigh and under my hand to rest over my throbbing core. His long fingers rest on the seam between my thighs, on jeans that are far too thick.

I undulate my hips, trying to generate friction between the jeans and my pulsing clit while Rif still kisses me. I fumble until I grip Jet's wrist, so bulky I can't close my fingers all the way around. I grind his hand against my clit. It isn't enough.

I break away from Rif to moan, "Please. More."

Jet presses on my clit with the heel of his hand, and it pulses in time with each pounding heartbeat. I climb a spiral coiling tighter inside me.

"Look at Jet, omega. Look at him while you ride his hand," Rif whispers in my ear as his palm curves over my breast. His thumb traces the peak on my top where my nipple is hard as rock.

My eyes fly open and I tumble into Jet's pitch-black depths. Something close to awe mixes with simmering heat that makes his eyes gleam like burnished onyx.

Jet holds me with his gaze as he increases the pressure. I rub myself against his fingers, going out of my mind, seeking sweet release, but I can only climb so far. Thick denim bars the way. I need more. I need his skin slipping through the obscene wetness between my legs.

Stef massages my breast with his large palm. Heat sears my skin as his crimson fingers tweak and pinch my hard nipple. I jolt with a streak of pain as Rif nudges his nose along my neck and licks a path from my collarbone to suck my earlobe into his mouth.

"Oh, God." Heat burns inside me, turning into an inferno. The tension turns again to pain and I cry out. I don't understand what's happening to me. My mind reels in confusion. Terror. Pain. Tears stream from my eyes. "Not enough."

"I will have to touch you more intimately, my omega. Say the words and I will do anything you ask," Jet says.

"Yes! Please, please, please touch me, Jet. I . . . I need you," I cry out, too far gone in my mind to care how I sound. My clothing is too tight, too restrictive. Suddenly, I hate the weight of my lab coat and the heaviness of my jeans. They have to go. Everything has to go. That way I can have their skin on mine, where it belongs.

"Ask us as our omega. Ask your alphas to provide what you want," Rif demands.

I quiver and wetness floods from my core; it's enough to wet my jeans through the crotch and down my thighs. It's like a river is gushing from me, accompanied by the sweet scent of apple blossoms.

Jet's nostrils flare. He leans down and drags his nose along the seam of my jeans, pulling the scent into his lungs. "Hells, omega. Your scent . . . this cunt . . ."

"I smell her, brother. She's intoxicating." The growl Stef emits is filled with fire. His fingers pinch my nipple. I suck in a quick breath as the coil knots my insides and squeezes.

"Ask us, omega. Ask your alphas to tend to your need," Rif growls.

I'm beyond words, beyond thought, but somehow, words I didn't conceive burst from me. "Please, alphas!"

I can't comprehend my words. They spring from a part of me that didn't exist before. I hear a ripping sound and cool air swirls around my hips and legs. I look down to see Jet sheer away my jeans with one of his sharp claws. His black eyes gleam as he stares at the place between my legs. Light-blue electricity crackles across his shoulders and down his arm to disappear into his skin.

"That's the hjerte bluss, brother," Stef exclaims, awe in his tone.

"That's how we know she's our true heart. Our mate." Jet's eyes glitter with pure possession, but I'm lost. Lost as his fingers find my core and slip between my folds.

I'm so wet he glides to my entrance and spears me with a thrust of his wrist. I throw back my head and arch my back as sensation shoots upward, too far gone to care how wanton I must look. My eyes roll back in my head as he works his finger inside me, strumming me as if I'm his favorite instrument.

I moan, gasping his name, concentrating on the pressure building between my legs. A second finger joins the first, and as he slides into me, he circles my clit with his thumb.

"Yes, yes, yes." I chant the word, losing myself behind closed lids as I climb toward the pinnacle.

I'm not a person who lets three men touch her at once. I don't let men touch me when I'm not emotionally invested, and that usually takes a long time. Weeks. Months. I'm not driven by my physical needs, and men are scared off by my intelligence long before I'm ready for anything intimate. They also don't enjoy taking second place to my lab and my research.

But these demons aren't men. They're something else and right now, I don't recognize the needy creature that has awoken inside me. That unrestrained part of myself where need and desire are stronger than the limits of my mind. They have unlocked something deep within me. Something buried so deep it wasn't a functional part of me. I've been taken apart and rearranged, and the dormant parts of myself have been made dominant.

And then nothing else matters when Jet thrusts into my core, curls his fingers inside me, and drags the tips somewhere that sets off sparks of pure sensation. He presses his thumb onto my clit and grinds down, giving me the release I need. My mouth falls open and Rif devours my scream with a searing kiss as I crest the peak. He thrusts his tongue inside my mouth, eating my release.

White dots spark behind my closed lids as my orgasm drags on. I am nothing as I soar, my climax so strong I lose myself in a wash of pure white. I drift back into my body to find their hands petting me. The air crackles again and electricity dances along their arms.

"So beautiful, omega. You're gorgeous when you cum. Your cunt gushes for us. Now I want to see the rest of the omega the heavens sent to us," Rif groans.

Cool air grazes my belly when he tears my top with a quick swipe of his hand. A flick of a lethal claw separates my bra, and all their hands still where before they'd stroked and patted me. There's nothing. No touches. No petting. Sweat prickles across my body and my skin burns. A whine works up my throat. The freshly awakened needy part of me doesn't understand why they stopped giving me the attention I'm so desperate for.

Jet's growl makes my skin pull tight. "Rif! Why did you not tell us she was so injured?"

"I was . . . her scent . . . Can you forgive me, omega?" Rif's deep voice vibrates through the fog clouding my mind.

Carefully they peel the rest of my ripped clothing off my body, revealing a mass of wounds. My collarbone grates where my shoulder hangs at an angle. Blood smears from seeping wounds, and all I can think is thank God whatever the reptile gave me still oozes through my body because I should be in a lot of pain with these injuries. This pain is different from the pain that seared through me when I yearned for their touch. Instead, the world has a hazy, floaty quality that I want to soak in forever. Then I won't have to make sense of anything.

"She needs the Orkneyjar," Jet says.

"Want . . . home," I say. I don't want this Orkneyjar. I want to wake up in my bed and sigh with relief when I realize this was some horrible dream my brain conjured up.

Rif surges to his feet, slips his arms beneath my shoulders and knees, and lifts me against his chest. I inhale his scent of leather and drag it into my lungs like a drug. "You are home. *We* are your home. The protectors who let you roam unattended don't deserve you. It's a loss they'll have to live with forever. They're never getting you back."

He strides into another room, the space resembling a cave made from smooth, dark rock. The black stone looks as though it has melted like lava and reformed like porcelain. The utilities are familiar. I note what looks like a sink, mirror, towels, and toilet. Steam rises from the bubbling water of a small pool in the corner.

Rif reaches along the band of the leather strips he wears and unlatches a clasp. The garment falls to the floor. He steps into the pool and lowers us. The effervescent water closes around us. Bubbles tickle my skin as he positions me between his long legs. He presses me so my back rests against his chest and I'm caged by his body.

His long, thick cock prods my back. It's a pure, solid mass which throbs when he tugs me close. Thick and meaty, it's a rock of engorged muscle, and there's no way I can ignore it. The sheer size of it can't be real, and yet the evidence is there against my back.

My heart kicks in my chest and my leaden limbs jerk. My fingers clutch the edge of the pool, and I try to pull myself away from him. It is futile, of course. With a languid press of his palm on my neck, I'm once again crushed against his firm body.

"No!" I gasp.

Rif nuzzles my ear, his lips drifting along my neck. "Relax, omega. These are the healing waters of the Orkneyjar. It comes from the deep waters of Amadon and replenishes our health. We'll rest here while you heal."

His enormous arms wind around my body, gently washing the blood and grime away. His touch is light as he skims his fingers over my arms, stomach, and legs. The water stains crimson before it is sucked away. A subtle current flows around me and follows the trail of blood to a corner of the pool, where it drains, leaving the water clear.

Jet and Stef strip and lower their massive bodies into the pool. The water hides their erect cocks and heavy balls set between muscular thighs, but the glimpse is enough to sear the impression against the inside of my skull. They're huge—long and thick—and my pussy clenches.

Stef leans toward me, never taking his gaze off me. I'm nothing but prey under the full focus of a predator, and that unrecognizable thing inside me preens under their attention. "When you're better, your omega heat will call to our alpha rut and we'll bond you to us forever. Our hearts will flare and our souls will fuse."

My focus slips from his fathomless black eyes to roam their bare chests, taking in defined muscles, rigid beneath smooth crimson skin. Their shoulders are broad and support arms that could bench-press an entire nation, with taut, bulging biceps that are thicker than my thighs.

From their temples, double horns rise above their skulls, curving and sweeping upward majestically, ending in a sharp point, while their lower horn curls to beneath their ears. The serrated edge of the upper horn looks like it could cut through a brick with the flick of their heads.

Jet's hair is white, striking against his crimson skin. It's so long it flows down his back like strands of pure silk. Two thick braids threaded with golden beads fall over his shoulders. Stef's hair is electric blue, with thicker strands falling halfway down his chest. The ends hit the water and swell around him.

My abdomen tightens into a cramp. I can't hide my wince. I grip my stomach as though that will help ease the pain, and it predictably fails.

"She needs us to touch her, brothers," Rif says.

"With pleasure." Jet slides along the pool toward me, and Stef takes my other side. Jet circles his large hand around my ankle and Stef ghosts his touch up my arm. Instantly the cramp eases and I relax against Rif, too exhausted to do anything but sink against him.

Rif pours some liquid into a brass goblet from a pitcher beside the pool and holds it to my lips. "Drink, omega. The waters can dehydrate, and you have a lot of healing to do."

He doesn't give me a choice and sets the goblet against my bottom lip. I open my mouth automatically, thinking how much of a bad idea it is to ingest anything, but the water is cool and I finish the whole goblet despite the slight metallic flavor that coats my mouth.

"Tell us how you came to be in the burning fields so I can bring your protectors to justice," Rif says.

The burning fields didn't properly describe the inferno I'd been thrown into. Maybe this really was hell and I had died. "No protectors."

Rif's growl vibrates through my back. "How can an omega have no protectors? That's unheard of. Which part of Amadon do you hail from?"

"Amadon?" I ask. My head is hazy and it's getting harder to think.

"You must come from one of the other six territories," Stef says.

He tilts my head, scoops the water from the pool with another jug, and pours it over my hair. He squirts a gel into his palm and works it through the strands. My body is instant liquid. My eyelids droop and I think I groan aloud, but I can't be sure. He works the gel into a lather, the tips of his claws scraping leisurely against my skull. A floral scent rises from the foam before he washes it out.

"No territory. From . . . my lab. There was a . . . sun flare." My mind ticks over, coming up with nothing because there's no way a sun flare could have sucked me up and thrown me out. It's impossible, and yet . . . I'm here. The water is warm and real. Rif's erect cock throbs against my back. That is most certainly real.

My eyelids part when a soft cloth passes across my foot. Jet crouches in front of me with my foot in his hand. He rubs the cloth gently over the arch and between my toes before swiping it up my calf.

"Why would an omega be in a lab?" Stef asks.

"She's obviously not been cared for as befits an omega," Rif says.

My body throbs, but not with the urgency of before when I'd been out of my mind with desire. Now it's beginning to fill with the full-blown terror I'd experienced when I'd found myself in geysers of flames. I was a lab rat. A brain. A means to an end. Never desired. I'm not this omega thing they think I am.

"My job. Important," I say. If I don't get back, the cells will perish and my latest results will be at risk. People will continue to die if I'm not there to harvest them. "Have to . . . get back."

Rif's eyes flare and harden. He slides a thick finger along my cheek until he cups my chin and tilts back my head so I have no choice but to look at him. The beads in his hair clink together and shroud me with his presence.

"My little omega, that's where you're wrong. You very much belong here and you are very much ours. Once you're healed and are strong enough to accept our claiming bites, you'll never be displaced again. You will understand that you belong to us and that, unlike your former protectors, we will never let you go."

Chapter Five

Stefnan

Our omega sleeps, but it's not restful. An omega in pre-heat should be soft and pliant in her slumber so her body can prepare for the rigors of full heat. Our omega should sleep especially deep because of her injuries and the energy it takes to heal through the waters of the Orkneyjar. Instead, our strange but beautiful omega moans and tosses her head. Beads of perspiration gather on her smooth forehead, and her pale brows knit.

At the very least, the Orkneyjar restored the injuries she sustained on her skin. My stomach hollows at the memory of the slashes all over her body and the fact we were so taken with finding her we didn't see them at first.

I'll spend years making that up to her. An omega as fragile as her should never have been in the healing fires scorching the land. She's tiny, even by the standards of omega in our species. I marvel at her slender limbs, the fine bones in her hands, and her pale skin so thin that in some places on her body, her veins are visible. I've never seen a female as alluring or special anywhere in the six territories.

As soon as I saw her, I knew she was ours, and when the *hjerte bluss* crackled over my body, I knew fate had finally smiled on us. The heart flare only combusts for true mates and signals the ultimate blessing from the fates. There is no doubt in my heart who she is to us, even though it's yet to flare for Rif and Jet.

This delicate female, wherever she is from, is our salvation for my bond brothers as well as Amadon.

"Do you think she feels the mate bond?" I murmur. The worry tastes bitter on my tongue because this female doesn't seem to understand any of this. They are awake as I am, quiet only because of our wonder.

"Perhaps D'Kali's serum affected her reaction to us," Rif says. If he's looking for excuses, then he's worried about her too. He traces her arm with a gentle caress, unable to stop touching her.

"It wasn't like this for the elders, was it?" I have to rely on their experience as I have none of my own.

Omegas are extremely rare. Alphas less so. Most of our people are beta born. For every four alphas, there is usually only one omega birth. Or that's the way it used to be. In our territory, no omega has been born for close to two decades. Without precious omega's there will be no alpha or omega born. Betas only give birth to betas. It's been a driving concern that soon, there will be no omega or alpha born at all. A whole part of our population will cease to exist.

My heart trips because my omega mother passed with The Death when I was little. My parents had only just formed their pack, and I was the result of my mother's first heat. Their one and only son. Before they could have any more children, my mother was torn from them in the next wave of sickness to strike the stronghold. My father's soon followed as is the way of losing a bond between alphas and their omega.

"They never mention resistance. Never," Stef says.

"It's the sign of finding a true mate, but perhaps it's different with her species," Jet says. He reaches across me and wipes the perspiration from her forehead with a cloth. She tosses her head and moans again.

"Where does she hail from?" Rif says.

I have to contain the sweep of rage shooting through me. I'm touched by a far greater urgency than anger. "Do you think she's from one of the other territories and lost her way?"

A more insidious idea pops to mind. What if she were taken and left there to die? She has no natural defenses, and the state she was in when Rif brought her to us was more than worrying. It would only have been a matter of time before the fires overcame her.

"She doesn't look like she's from another territory," Jet says.

She lacks wings, scales, claws, or any of the features needed to survive. Each species has the characteristics to live in the other six territories.

"They're secretive. Perhaps they've hidden their omegas from us," Rif says.

"We're at war. It's not like they're going to be forthcoming with any information, especially about omegas. They'd rather see us die out than hand over their greatest treasures." Jet's black eyes flash with anger.

Our lands have been fighting for as long as I've been alive, and what he says is true. Without omega, there will be no more alphas or omegas born. Our generation of alphas is one of the last. Our world is changing, and it isn't for the better. It leaves us defenseless from attacks from other planets, and since the Solice War six generations ago where more than half our world's population was wiped out, we're still suffering.

"She is reacting to us. She's in pre-heat at least, which is progress. We'll do everything in our power so she fully accepts us as mates," Rif says.

"You can't hammer a round peg into a square hole, Rif," I say.

He lifts eyes filled with the heavy burden of the Alpha Prime Warlord of Rjúkaland. "If we don't, we risk losing her. I'll not have that, Jet. I'll do anything. To save her is to save us—our lives and our territory."

I nod my head, because we're on the same side. Desperation fills his words. "I'm with you, brother, but don't push her away in your haste."

Unless she's in full heat, we can't bond her. Until then, there's a chance she'll get away from us, and I'll never let that happen. I'll do everything within my power to keep her. If it takes orgasm after orgasm, I'll gladly give her my mouth, my tongue, my hands, and my cock. It won't be a hardship. Even now my cock is swelling with the need to be inside my omega. My mouth waters at the thought of her taste. Of her swollen folds and the river of slick she'll gush for me. I'll drink from her forever and take no other sustenance if she'll let me.

The door opens and D'Kali strides in. I frown, rising onto my elbow to protect my omega from his sight. He of all beings should know better than to disturb us. He's long-lived enough to have been one of the original Ulgix who saved our race from the interstellar attacks of the Solice Wars and seen firsthand how protective alphas are of their omegas. It's difficult to ignore the fire that runs through my blood at his intrusion. "What do you want, D'Kali? Our omega sleeps."

I make sure our omega is covered with a blanket. She fell asleep after the healing waters. We'd carefully dried her and lain with her to rest in Rif's sleeping quarters, all of us unable to return to our usual duties in case she needed us.

D'Kali stops short at my tone. His face hardens but he recovers quickly, folding his hands in front of him and wringing his fingers. "My apologies, warlord."

My eyes narrow because he doesn't seem apologetic, but then our omega stirs. Her strange and beautiful eyes flutter open. I'm unprepared for their exotic color to fall on me. They're so light blue, it reminds me of the midday sky. I'm lost in her gaze until she gasps and they harden with terror.

Her gaze pings over all of us before it lands and stays on D'Kali. Her breath becomes shallow rasps. "Get away from me!"

She tries to crawl away from us, but Rif, Jet, and I have caged her in. She has nowhere to go.

"It's okay, omega. We won't hurt you," I say.

My words have no effect. She clasps the sheets at her chest and balls her body against the wall at the head of the bed. "I want to go home."

Her words spear my heart. "You are home. We'll take care of you. Cherish you. You are ours to protect now. That's not a duty we'll take lightly," Jet says. I can tell he's worried too.

He reaches for her, but she pulls away from him with a sharp tug. "Don't touch me!"

"If I may?" D'Kali says.

Rif snarls. "What is it?"

She flinches and whines at Rif's harsh tone. She looks so small between us. She should feel protected by our much larger bodies, but she's not from here. Perhaps where she's from, they mistreat omegas and that's why trust doesn't come easily for her.

"I can determine her species," D'Kali says. There's something hard about the way he trains his gaze on her. I've known D'Kali all my life, as did my parents and their parents, and I've never mistrusted his judgment. But I've never had an omega before, either.

"I'm human. From . . . Earth. Where . . ." Her throat bobs and she takes a shaky breath. "Where am I?"

A human? From Earth? I've never heard of such a planet or her species, let alone how she could have arrived here. My blood runs cold, and I share a look with both Rif and Jet. The Ulgix assured us we were safe from interplanetary threat. Our alpha warriors have dwindled to a precariously low number, and betas aren't strong enough to fend off an attack.

"You're in Rjúkaland on Amadon, little omega. Safe from the healing fires," Rif says in a bid to keep the omega settled. A settled omega is one who will slip into heat.

"Stop calling me this omega thing. I'm a person. A woman. My name is Adele. I'm a human being, and I definitely don't belong here." Her chest heaves. I ache to bring her into my arms and comfort her, but I don't think she'll let me.

"Omega . . ." Jet says.

Her blue eyes dart to him, flashing and angry. I can't help the rush of amusement that runs through me. She has a temper. That will go a long way to keep Rif in line. No one else has authority or power over him, but this tiny female has him wrapped around her dainty little finger.

She clutches the sheets so tight her knuckles turn white. "I demand to go back home. I don't belong here. There has to be a way . . ." Her pale brows furrow and draw together. She mutters a stream of words under her breath. I catch the words "sun flare" and "impossible" and "something out of a sci-fi movie." Whatever that is.

"The omega is agitated. Perhaps another dose of serum will pacify her," D'Kali says.

The omega looks up, her gaze searing. "My name is Adele, and don't you dare inject me with anything again."

"She's upset. I advise we take her to my lab to test for The Death. We don't want the disease to spread to another species," D'Kali says. "We don't want her to waste away as did your omega mothers."

Dread spears through me, almost immobilizing me with fear. I don't want our omega to die like my mother and all the other omegas The Death has taken.

"Rest is the most important thing for our omega . . ." Rif says.

"Adele. My name is Adele," our omega says. Her grip on the blanket is still white-knuckled, but her shoulders rise into a tight line.

"Anger isn't healthy for her, Rif." I gather her in my arms, holding her naked body in the sheet, and I ignore the way she struggles to free herself. She should know she doesn't have to struggle for anything again. When these humans lost her, they forfeited all rights to her.

"D'Kali is right. We need to make sure she hasn't contracted The Death before she goes into heat. If she were to get pregnant, I shudder to think what could happen if she contracted the disease," I say.

She pushes my shoulder in a playful shove, but when I look down at her, her eyes are flinty and her features stretch tight. Ah, it wasn't a playful shove, but she isn't very strong. "I'm not going. Put me down!"

"Your care is of utmost importance, which we'll ensure, even if you don't understand that yet," I say.

Her mouth falls open in an adorable pout, and her next inhale is noisy. She kicks her legs. They bump into my hip, doing no harm to my tough hide, and I only hope she doesn't damage herself. She's a pleasant weight in my arms as I walk from Rif's quarters and into the stronghold proper.

A thrill goes through me when I make a mental note to order space made for our omega's nest. She'll need a selection of materials to choose from where she can make her nest and invite us in. My cock swells in anticipation. I never thought I'd have the chance of falling into rut with an omega, let alone *my* omega. The one omega my heart flare crackles into life for.

The omega stills her struggles and looks at our surroundings as we stride along the corridors. They're sturdy. Made from petrified Fyette wood, burned into the hardest substance after the healing fires have passed through the trees. They're straight and solid, standing vertically and joined to great planks with solid steel bolts.

Betas scurry from our path. Our omega's head pivots as she takes everything in. When she's well-rested and with young after her heat, I'll take great pride in showing her around her new home. While her scent fragrances the air, especially sweet and potent in her pre-heat, she'll need to be contained. Even betas will scent her. I'll not have her share it. Her scent belongs only to us.

I take her downstairs, deep below the ground, to D'Kali's lab. It's as different here as night is to day. We step into a blindingly white, sterile room with unnatural light and technology built for the Ulgix. The fine hairs on the back of my neck rise whenever I come into this room, which I do regularly for D'Kali to check that I'm healthy. It's a prerequisite of all alphas for the protection of our planet. Without alpha warriors, betas are not strong enough on their own should we need to protect our population.

"This . . . is a lab?" the omega questions. Her brow furrows and she casts a gaze around the room. She ceases her struggles and instead is compliant in my arms.

"Put her on the gurney," D'Kali says and moves to collect his equipment. Several Ulgix dressed in white coats bustle around, assisting him.

My omega stiffens in my arms when she sees the lab table D'Kali indicated. "I'm not going on that thing."

It's a sterile piece of equipment and I don't blame her. "Don't worry, omega. You'll be safe in my arms."

I sit on it. The metal is cold on the backs of my thighs but soon warms. I'm used to the table and the straps that are sometimes used when we need treatment that is particularly painful. I wouldn't expect the same for my omega.

D'Kali approaches her with an instrument. He darts in and holds it to her arm. I hiss when she jerks. "Seek permission before you approach my omega, D'Kali."

"My apologies, alpha," he says.

My omega rubs her arm and shoots D'Kali a narrow-eyed look. "He's not sorry at all."

I track D'Kali as he moves to his equipment and loads her blood into his computers. My omega gasps when a hologram appears above her body. She looks up at it, probably as intrigued as I am whenever I see these images appear in mid-air.

D'Kali lifts his hand to the diagram and spins it, humming to himself. The image floats in mid-air and turns as he commands. It's transparent and made from many colors. I'm at a loss to understand what it means, however complex it is.

"This is my blood," my omega murmurs.

My brow tightens into a frown. I look at her, but she locks her attention on the hologram. Her hand darts out and flips the hologram, as D'Kali did. She tweaks her fingers and enlarges part of the diagram.

"You understand the illustrations?" Jet asks.

"They're blood cells. Human," she says and points. "See? There's a mix of red and white blood cells and platelets. Animals have hemocytes. I don't know what you have unless I can study your blood work, but—"

"That's not for you to touch, omega," D'Kali says.

He moves toward our omega, and Jet quickly steps between the Ulgix and our female. He growls and the sound reverberates around the room. The lab assistants freeze, and all faces turn to us.

My omega jostles in my arms as something in the hologram catches her attention. "Look!"

Rif crosses his arms over his chest. His brows drop low over his eyes. "What is it, omega?"

She turns her pale face toward him before sectioning off part of the hologram. "My blood cells should be donut-shaped to allow them to trickle into the tiniest blood vessels, but these are . . ." She looks back at the shapes I can see quite clearly are not round. "These are disfigured. These spiky projections indicate . . . methylmercury in my system. How can that be?"

I stare at Rif, at a loss. I don't understand what she means.

Her forehead beads with sweat. She swipes it away with a distracted flick of her hand. "Even if they weren't misshapen, the green glow gives it away," she says.

She's becoming agitated, squirming on my lap. Her pale face is growing white as all the color leaches from her cheeks. "This level should be impossible. No fish. No external exposure. No metallic contact. Ingestion . . . It only takes twenty-four hours for mercury to affect the blood." Her words taper away and her gaze flicks to D'Kali, hardening.

"She's growing restless. She needs more serum to calm her," D'Kali says. He opens a drawer and removes an injector I recognize. It's no different from those he uses to treat all of us when we're in pain. Tension runs through her body. I band my arms around her.

She holds out her hand, palm toward the Ulgix, and reels into my chest. "Don't come near me with that thing."

A nameless expression flashes across his face, come and gone in a second. If I weren't watching, I would have missed it. "You need to be calm, omega."

Rif breaks into a purr. Her eyelids flutter and she fights them closing. "No. Don't want . . . that sound . . ."

She groans and clasps her abdomen as a cramp overcomes her. This isn't good for her pre-heat. Her body is already under an enormous state of stress, and her reaction to D'Kali isn't helping. My instinct is deep and ingrained. My purr joins with Rif, both of us needing to provide comfort for our omega.

"No . . . please," she whispers. She fights the relaxed state that's a gift from alphas to their omegas. Jet joins in our chorus and her eyes drift shut. She slumps against my chest, her body burning with heat. She twists and mutters in her sleep. Her head moves as she fights our purrs instead of letting it comfort her. Even in her alpha-induced relaxed state, she resists us.

My instinct rises within me, fast and overwhelming. We need to bond our omega before she can resist us anymore. And before we get to the mystery of why she understands D'Kali's technology and thinks she's been poisoned.

I lock my gaze with my bond brothers, gathering her in my arms and tucking her against my chest. We've known each other all our lives, and this is one of those times we don't need words because we're all thinking the same thing. "We have to bond her and we must do it as fast as we can."

"I agree," Jet says, his deep purr echoing in the room.

"I'm not losing our omega. We'll just have to fuck the fight out of her first and force her from pre-heat into full heat. We'll seek her forgiveness after we've bonded," Rif says.

I shove aside the pit of snakes writhing in my belly. We'll be taking away her choice. Yet Rif is correct—it's the only thing we can do in these circumstances.

Chapter Six

Adele

I drift through warm layers, realizing the demons sent me to sleep again with their deep, rumbling purrs. Only, they're not demons. They're... *aliens*. I'm not dead or in hell or on Earth.

I'm *on another planet*.

I slam into full wakefulness. We're back in the room, on the large bed the massive alien—Rif—brought me into. All three touch me, their large, terrifying hands curved around my arm, my hip, my calf.

We're all tangled in smooth sheets, but acres of their crimson flesh are visible. My focus draws to their bulging biceps and carved chests with pecs that are more slabs than sections of muscle, and torsos that are chiseled washboards capable of grating a sponge. Shadowed dips and hard ridges disappear into black sheets that hide too much from me.

An inner consciousness stirs within me, swift and possessive, and it steals my mind. A beast with a mind of her own. I want to see all of them laid out bare to me. On offer for me only. Their bodies are mine, for my pleasure. My right to own. Their hands, their backs, their cocks, their seed.

A wave of heat slams through me and perspiration breaks out on my skin. My stomach twists and a gush of warm liquid spills from my core. A sweet apple-blossom fragrance colors the air. Fire licks my veins, burning with need. I need my alphas. Liquid desire streams through me and my hand drifts between my thighs, seeking the heat of my core. I'm soaking wet. There's a puddle beneath me, making the black sheets shine. I've flooded the sheets and any embarrassment I endure is immediately shoved aside by a new part of myself. I'm not embarrassed. I'm happy. Needy. Achy. A languid throb rolls through me.

I'm ready for my alphas.

Ready for them to take me. Fuck me. Breed me and—

No! What . . . what am I thinking? My stomach twists again for a different reason. I don't understand why I'm like this.

Omega.

They said I was an omega.

My knowledge about omegas centers around wolves. The omega is at the bottom of the hierarchy of wolf pack society, but the way they look at me with hunger in their eyes suggests something far greater than animal instincts.

Or maybe it's about animal instincts and they're acting out of a biological need and now so am I. But how? I've never been like *this*. Biological creatures adapt to their environment. The shape of a beak, type of feet, position of eyes, development of whiskers, the sharpness of teeth—structural adaptations developed for survival.

I've come here, altered into something else. Myself, but not. I've adapted through being broken down and reconstructed across time and space. An endless pit opens deep inside me and I plummet off a mental cliff into an abyss.

I'm a creature of instinct, my body primed for sex. My body is now the perfect vessel to breed.

Yes. The new part of me agrees, but the old part of me, the rational part holding on by her fingernails, screams her denial.

I sit up, breath sharp, and turn to the large open window and balcony where the flying horse on fire brought me. The sky is bright crimson, fading to yellow along the horizon. Black wispy clouds smudge the flawless vignette, but nothing like the thick black clouds that stole the sky when I found myself torn from my lab and thrown into this hell.

The beast screams at me to wake her alphas. She needs them to quench the fire licking through her blood. Instead, I untangle myself from the sheets, carefully wriggling from beneath their massive hands. Hands that touch me so gently and carefully, despite their size. Despite having the strength to crush my skull.

It doesn't matter how gentle they are. They want something from me because I'm this omega that I never agreed to change into. I don't want to be here. I want to be back in my lab, finding a cure for the cancer time bomb in my body.

Jet's fingers flex when I remove my calf from his grip, and I let out a sigh of relief when he stays asleep. I extricate myself from the bed and turn my back to them. The creature in me hisses her displeasure, but I force my feet away from them. I'm stronger than she is. I have to be.

A breeze floats in from the open doorway and cools the perspiration from my overheated skin. I find a discarded shirt on the floor and haul it over my body. Sandalwood wafts around me, calming me. I tell myself it's because I'm no longer naked and not because this is Jet's shirt.

I skim my fingers over my forearm. My skin is smooth. I check my legs, finding them unmarred from the hundreds of nicks I received from the bladed plants. I haven't any scientific explanation for that, so I turn my focus to the open doorway and ledge.

I step into the sun and make my way across the landing to clutch the banister. It's high, coming to my mid-chest, but I can still see what's stretched below me.

It's a scene straight out of a medieval movie, only nothing about this is as tame as a movie. Giant logs with massive carved points frame the village laid out beneath me. Paved streets line rows of joined thatched houses. Figures mill in the streets, walking, chatting, yelling after children darting beneath the taller legs of adults. Muffled sounds of life float to me, along with the vague smells of food, musky hints of animals, and the taint of garbage.

They look like my demons, with red skin and horns, but from my vantage point I can see they are smaller and certainly not anywhere near as muscular. Their horns are diminutive and curve around the backs of their heads. I scan the crowd, looking for double horns with wicked serrated edges, and come up short. Then, marching in a small group, I spot a triad of double-horned demons, but they still lack the sheer body mass of my alphas.

My alphas . . .

No. *They're not*. They're aliens who want to quiet me, make me soft and compliant with the hypnotic rumbles I succumb to every time they start.

It's not only them. There's the reptile creature who I'm sure is poisoning me. The transition of the lab they took me to compared to the rustic medieval room and village spread beyond is jarring. Almost as though two different cultures exist together, but they aren't melding. I scan the village, the huge spiked pylons in the distance, and turn to the room I'm stuck in.

It's lived in and comfortable. There's a pile of cushions, a couch, and rugs on the floor. There's no technology. Nothing from the lab. The lighting is natural, or from wood fires. There's no transport other than beasts of burden. No sounds of anything electronic. There are two very distinct separate cultures here.

There's nothing similar to my home.

To . . . Earth.

A desperate wave of wretchedness slams into me with the force of a tsunami. I want my lab. My apartment. The research I spent hours of back-breaking work on. The time I spent over a microscope, harvesting cells, doing experiment after experiment. Working through the failures. Begging for funding, training assistants, giving up anything resembling a social life. I gave up friends. Boyfriends. My lab was my life. I was doing something important. I was saving lives. I was . . .

I . . . I can't stay here.

My chest constricts. I try to breathe and I can't. Nothing goes into my airways, no matter how hard I try. My heart's racing and I'm sweating for a different reason than the inferno that's surging within me. The world spins as I dig my fingernails into the hard wooden banister I'm leaning against for support.

"Omega!" The scent of sandalwood hits me. Warm arms surround me. A large hand cups my nape and crushes me against a hard chest. The creature in me forces me to smoosh my nose into his skin. My chest loosens and I drag in lungfuls of air tainted with his scent. Golden beads clink, and the ends of his long braids tickle my cheek.

Jet. Alpha. Protect. Love. Cherish. Home.

The human part of my mind balks. I try to push away, but with a flex of his muscles, I'm locked in place with no effort on his behalf. I'm no match for his strength. "Let me go!"

"No, omega. You're distressed." His chest rumbles to life and my muscles immediately turn to jelly.

"Stop that!" I gasp before it can lull me into complacency again. That's a dangerous place to be. My defenses are down, giving the thing in me a chance to surface.

"But you're anxious," Jet says as his brow lowers.

"I don't care! I have every right to be. Just . . . stop it!" I screech, pulling the last ounce of my reserves into the words.

His chest falls silent. I glance up into his black eyes as they flare. "It's only to comfort you, omega. My fathers often comforted my mother by purring."

Purr. So that's what they call that sound. At least he stopped when I asked. He still has me locked tight against his supple, velvety-leather skin. Ridges appear on his shoulders, slight scale-like patterning adding an extra layer of protection. Everything about this male screams predator. "I'm not your mother. I don't like your purr."

His brow furrows. "Omegas find their alpha mates' purr comforting. It's an alpha's honor to provide it. You'll need us to purr for you when you're in estrus. I won't have you in pain, omega."

My belly quivers with the sound of his deep voice. It's rumbly, like the purr. I'm on the cusp of leaning into him. Of telling him not to mind what I just said. To purr for me because it *is* comforting. Anesthesia for my mind.

My mind snags on one word, and ice floods my system. "Estrus?"

"Estrus will follow your pre-heat, which you're in now. The cramps will get worse. You'll feel like your blood is boiling. You'll crave your alphas. You'll beg for us. Our purrs. Our cocks. We'll gladly offer it all to you. You'll beg for our seed."

Every muscle in my body seizes, and my hands clamp around his massive biceps. "Never." My whisper is harsh, as though I'm trying to convince myself.

"We'll always provide you with the utmost pleasure. All of us. At any time. You don't need to be afraid," Jet says.

My gaze slides to Rif and Stef, who still sleep. I don't know how I fit on the bed with the three of them, but I don't think I've ever slept so well either. That doesn't matter. None of it matters because Jet just told me they plan to fuck me when I'm in this estrus.

My tongue sticks to the top of my mouth. I shake my head, as though denying everything will make it go away. It's childish, but it's all I've got. Another cramp twists my abdomen and, trying not to give in to it, I dig my fingernails into his skin. "I'm a human. Not an omega. Humans don't enter estrus. They don't have heats. Whatever you think I am, you're wrong."

Chapter Seven

Adele

"Omega..." Jet starts.

I clench my teeth and ignore the flames prickling under my skin. "Adele. My name is Adele. Not omega. I'm a scientist. My work is too important, so I can't stay here. I need to go home."

Jet's fingers soothe a path down my spine. He starts to purr but shuts it down. I should be grateful he remembered, but another cramp hits and I gasp, folding in half. Jet picks me up, takes me inside, and places me back on the bed. His large hand cups my face while his other hand holds my shoulder. He looms over me, knees on either side of my legs. "Let me soothe you. Let me help."

I grip his wrist. I want to push him away, but I can't. Where his skin touches mine is the absence of pain. "I want to go home. Please let me go home."

Rif stirs, his black eyes blinking open and immediately finding mine. He comes up onto his elbow and places his hand over my hip. On my other side, Stef stirs and wakes as uncannily fast as Rif. I'm the sole focus of all three aliens. My nipples peak and throb as the creature inside me rears up again, and I resist the urge to arch my back and thrust my breasts into their mouths.

"Her pre-heat is progressing," Jet says.

Rif's gaze floats over me and his fingers flex. "You'll feel better when you're bred, omega."

Fear strikes a blade through my heart. Heat. Estrus. Breed. The words fire arrows into my walled-up fear-center. My whole life has been dedicated to finding a cure for cancer. I've never wanted a child to suffer the same fate as myself. Heat of a different kind flickers over my skin so hot it leaves red splotches on my skin. "I don't want a baby."

"That's what all omegas want. It's ingrained," Stef says, rising on my other side. I'm walled in by acres of crimson muscle and unyielding intent.

They move in closer to me as I try to wiggle away. I have to think fast. They're not listening to me or what I want, so I aim for what will affect them. "I can't go into estrus. It would be too dangerous. The mercury poisoning in my blood would kill a baby if I were to fall . . . pregnant."

I'd never have a child, knowing their fate. That they'd have a higher-than-normal chance of developing cancer and die at a young age. What sort of monster would I be?

Knowing that didn't stop the part of me that did long for a child. But that's all it would ever be. A longing. A wish never to be realized.

"You said that before. What's mercury?" Jet asks, his brow creasing.

I guess they don't know exactly what mercury is, going by their lack of reaction to the DNA strand and three-dimensional cellular hologram of my blood work in the lab. "It's a chemical element." My mind ticks through mercury poisoning. Deaths have resulted from three months' exposure to diethyl mercury. The lethal dose of methylmercury is estimated to be two hundred milligrams, with paresthesia of the hands, feet, and mouth occurring at a total body burden of forty milligrams. There's no way of telling how much mercury was in my blood work, but the fire raging through me doesn't match up with what I know are the effects of mercury poisoning.

I also don't know where mercury could have come from, other than that injection. The chance of me developing mercury poisoning in my lab is extremely low, but I've ingested water and food here, and the reptile injected me with something I've had a reaction to. That serum is bad news.

Rif's eyes flare and his body goes rigid. His weighted focus lands on Stef and Jet. "Do you think it's The Death?"

"I don't know what this Death is, but mercury poisoning is lethal to humans," I say. "That's why I have to get home. If I stay here, I'll die."

That is the truth. Whether from the mercury poisoning or being boiled alive by the relentless heat burning me from the inside out is yet to be seen.

"We'll take her to D'Kali," Rif says.

"No! Not him." I stifle a shudder. In reality, they could do anything to me and there's nothing I could do.

"You don't like D'Kali," Rif says. He reaches across to trail a fingertip along my jaw, turning my head to look at him. His touch leaves a fiery wake, and the shiver I stifled is reborn. This one I can't hold in.

I don't like D'Kali. I don't trust him either, but nothing I think matters to them. *They* trust D'Kali. Maybe blindly. I don't understand why they have a highly technological lab beneath their medieval castle, but something about the reptile definitely has my guard up. I don't know what to say, though. To them, I'm nothing but a body to breed, my will ignored in the face of their own needs, while they know and trust D'Kali.

I have to wonder why. I'm human, and they're . . . not. I'm not even their species. Surely they'd want an omega who wants them in return—who wants to be owned, bred, fucked by them all.

At the same time?

The thought doesn't repel me as it should. Instead, the creature flies from the place I'd held her down, bringing with her liquid fire in my blood.

Another cramp seizes me and I cry out. I grip my belly, but it does nothing to relieve the violent spasm. A gaping emptiness opens deep inside me, and wetness seeps from between my legs. Sweet apple blossom rises around me. I'm so empty. I need to be filled. My pussy flutters, the sensation drilling up inside me until it slits my skull.

I lick my lips, my gaze drifting down Jet's body still above me on his hands and knees. My pussy throbs when my eyes find his cock thickening between his solid thighs. His cock swings upward until the head touches his abdomen. So thick. So lovely. I ache to circle my fingers around it. Wetness seeps from the slit at its head, and a pearly bead slides down his fiery length. Such a waste of his seed. It should be in me, filling the yawning emptiness.

Rif and Stef bolt upright, muscles straining. Their combined scents of sandalwood, cedar, and leather make my mouth water. I want to taste them—their skin, their sweat, their cum. Rif's hand glides across my breast and clamps down hard, eliciting a moan from the creature deep inside me. He finds my nipple between his thumb and forefinger and pinches. The slight pain is sweet relief.

"We can take away your pain, omega," Jet says. His breath is warm on my face. His lips are so close. If I tilt my chin, I could let him devour me.

"Tell Jet you don't want to leave us. That you want to stay as our omega. To be treasured as the precious female you are," Rif says.

Clarity spears the haze in my mind. The creature hisses as I focus on the thread of lucidity and ignore the fire in my blood. It's simmering in my peripheral, but it's manageable. I draw moisture into my mouth and force the words out, even though they're a tremulous whisper. "I want to go home. Please. Let me go home. "

Jet freezes. His eyes are lit with an inner fire as he draws a deep breath. "We're your alphas. We understand what you need when you need it. This is your home. We're your home. It's up to us to make you understand it."

His lips slam onto mine. His tongue delves into my mouth, and I'm consumed with the taste of sandalwood. The creature roars back to life. Our tongues duel. He takes, and it's all I can do to give in to what he demands. My legs fall apart. My thighs are slick, my pussy throbbing with need. I cant my hips, rising from the bed. I need . . . I want . . . his cock. I mewl into his mouth, clasping his cheeks with both hands, holding him to me as I try desperately to get his length between my legs.

He lowers his hips, sliding his cock through my slippery folds. The mushroom head strokes my clit. He grinds down with his body weight, his cock the perfect abrasion. Glorious sparks of sensation overcome me as a climax plows through me with total disregard for any arguments I have.

Jet roars. Electricity flashes up his arms and over his shoulders. Sparks jump onto my skin, but they only tickle instead of burn. I'm too far gone to be worried electricity has spontaneously combusted his body.

His cock pulses and covers my belly with wet heat. His scent intensifies. I drag it into my lungs as I soar. The creature inside me claims a chunk of my mind, stabbing me with claws that will never retract.

I sink back into my mind as Jet rises. He plasters his palm over his cum and rubs it into my belly. Rif takes one hand above my head while Stef holds my other. I'm spread and helpless beneath Jet as he draws his fingers through the mess on my belly. His cum pools in my belly button and runs down my hips. The sheet beneath me is awash with fluids. "This is exactly what you need, omega. Feel my seed fill your pores. Feel me seep into you. Feel me entering your bloodstream. Becoming you."

His cum dissolves into my skin as though I'm drinking him. My blood fizzes and my veins sweep it away. I do feel him inside my entire body, pumping through me with my rapid heartbeats. The creature in me hums with pleasure, appeased.

Jet puts his cum-stained finger to my mouth and forces it between my lips. Sandalwood explodes on my tongue, and I suck on the digit like a lollipop. I'm caught in his weighted stare, unable to pull my gaze from his as I continue to suck. "Good omega. Drink me in. My bond brothers will mark you next. Soon you'll have all three of us in your system. There'll be no confusion in your mind that you're ours and you're here to stay. Soon you'll know exactly who you belong to."

Chapter Eight

Adele

Jet's cum is delicious. Licking it from his finger is good, but I want it directly from the source. My gaze drifts down his body to where his cock is trapped between our hips. The head peeks out between our clamped abdomens. I tilt my hips, grinding myself against him because my hands are secured above my head.

"Uh-uh, omega. It's Stef's turn to give you your treat now," Jet says. He lifts himself away from me. I cry out when my skin tightens without the weight of his body pressing me down. My whole being is sensitive and overheated. The only parts of myself that feel as though they aren't on fire are my wrists where Rif and Stef hold me.

Stef lets me go and I almost cry out in anticipation of the pain, but Rif grabs hold of both my arms so I can't move. Jet moves around Stef with an agility that belies their large bodies, and before internal fire can lick my body, Jet lies next to me, and Stef takes his place between my splayed thighs.

A grin lights his face as he licks my seam with a long, slippery, and tensile tongue. The tip comes to a point and delves between my cheeks. I jolt as he laps my rosebud and cry out when he swirls my clit.

"Delicious," he murmurs.

He drops his head and devours my core. His tongue laves my tender flesh, and his lips tease and suck. He spears my pussy with his tongue as he sucks my folds. Still holding my wrists, Rif takes one breast in his mouth while Jet sucks at the other. Their hot tongues spark an explosion. My back arches. My muscles seize and my breath sticks in my lungs. I throw my head back into the pillow as an orgasm hurtles through me. I spiral up and up. The creature in me sighs with satisfaction, happy she's the full focus of her alphas. I'm too replete to argue with her as I drift down.

I collapse onto the bed, panting, looking down my body to where Stef swirls my clit with his tongue. Rif and Jet pop from my breasts, leaving the peaks rigid and cooling in the air. Stef's fangs peek from beneath his glistening lips. He scours the flat of his tongue over my sensitive seam as though he's licking his favorite flavored ice cream cone.

"I agree, brother." He glances at Jet, then back down at me. "She tastes divine."

His voice is a low rumble that makes my abdomen tighten. Wetness seeps from my core. Stef's nostrils flare and his eyes gleam. "Her slick smells good enough to eat."

"What's . . . slick?" I manage to make my wooly tongue pliable enough to speak.

Stef crawls up my body. His face is a mask of need and desire, his eyes liquid with arousal. "Your slick is manna from the gods. It's an omega offering for her alphas, showing them how much she needs her alphas to tend to her needs."

I shake my head. The slick coming from me is disgusting. I barely get wet enough for penetration. Usually. The few times I've had intercourse have been with the dab hand of a good lubricant. What was pouring from me is a viscous fluid that should be impossible. "Not omega. No slick."

I grunt when a cramp coils in my stomach, strong enough to threaten to petrify my muscles. The pain and the fire burn without their touch and the needy thing in me whines, impatient. A low growl seeps from me and I writhe.

"She needs your seed, brother. Don't make her wait," Rif growls.

Stef kisses me. His tongue flicks inside my mouth. I taste myself on him. Tangy and sweet feminine musk combined with pure apple-blossom sugar and his woody cedar scent. It's intoxicating. Potent. I moan and suck on his tongue, torn between disgust and rapture. He pulls back, looming over me while I chase him for more of a taste. "That's definitely slick, omega."

"No." The word is molasses, tasting of a lie. I still deny it.

I have to.

"You need a little more convincing, I see," Rif says. Quick as lightning, his hands clamp about my waist and I'm lifted into the air.

Stef dives under me onto his back, his body pinned beneath me as Rif settles me over his hips. A full-body shiver works through me when his cock sits in my folds. Stef's fingers curve over my hips, holding me in place. The thing inside me revels in being the sole focus of his stare.

Rif's hands snake to where Stef and I intimately touch. His fingers stroke through my seam, between Stef's engorged cock and my folds. His fingers glisten as he traces a path up Stef's abdomen. My slick leaves a silvery trail before he rubs it around Stef's nipple.

"Give him a lick, omega. Let your alpha feel your tongue on him and taste yourself again. It will help," Rif says.

Apple blossom fills my senses as the scent from me rises. I rub my finger in the substance Rif took from me. It's syrupy and clear. A liquid that I know isn't natural lubrication. This is something else.

Jet's hand clamps around my neck. "Taste yourself on your alpha. See how our flavors blend to perfection."

I'm drawn down. I don't need Jet guiding me as I willingly clamp my lips around his black nipple. Stef's scent mingles with mine. I moan, dragging my tongue over his nub. I don't realize I've moved my hips and am grinding myself against his rigid length before he shudders.

"Gods . . . feels so good." Stef's fingers flex and dig into my curves. They might leave bruises, but I'm too far gone to care.

He pushes up as his cock slides through my wet heat. The iron bar of his cock sends delicious thrills through me. I suck his nipple and grind myself against him. My legs widen, my knees gliding apart so I'm balanced on his length.

Rif's hand slides to my throat, turning my head to the side. An angry whine erupts from me. He's taken me away from the delicious taste of our melded scent before he pops his finger into my mouth.

I latch on, sucking my flavor mixed with leather as his finger drags on my tongue. My hips piston and I make a slippery mess between us that coats Stef's abdomen and my thighs, but I don't care. This is too good to stop, and my head fills with the dream-like haze again.

"Your body is learning the taste and touch of your alphas. We'll teach you everything you need to know before your heat takes over." Rif's voice vibrates along the shell of my ear. I shudder as more slick gushes out of me, scenting the air with my out-of-control lust.

Stef audibly draws in air and he smashes his cock against my clit. I scream when an orgasm barrels through me. I clamp down on Rif's finger as Stef's fingers dig into me. His hips work and his cock creates friction that shoots me into the stratosphere.

He groans in my ear. His length pulses and heat spurts against my abdomen, coating both of us. Stef reaches between us, scooping a handful of his cum and stuffing it into my mouth.

The creature in me hisses in ecstasy as the fluid coats my mouth and drips down my throat. I can't get enough. I lick his hand, eager for more. He doesn't disappoint me, scooping up more for me to sip. I gulp it down, licking his palm and sucking his fingers. Our essences coat my chin and my cheeks. I don't care. I want to smell like them. I want to be owned by them. I want everyone to know who these alphas belong to.

"Let your other alpha satisfy your hunger." Jet eases me to sit on Stef's still iron-hard cock.

Rif turns my head. He's kneeling on the bed next to me, stroking his cock. I'm transfixed as he palms his girth and the strange ring around the base that sits tight to his abdomen. He grips the base tightly enough that his knuckles whiten. "This is all for you. You'll be the first and last to have my knot."

"Knot?" My fuzzy brain doesn't connect what he's saying. My gaze falls back to his cock, transfixed by the slightly darker ring of skin. The part of my brain that is still operating gasps in shock because at some stage they'll want to put their cocks in me and holy hell, I don't know how that thing is going to fit in me.

"Our knots will inflate when we breed you and seal us together when we give you our seed. One of the greatest gifts an alpha can give their omega," Stef says. His electric-blue hair falls over his face, but I still see how his eyes burn.

My brain short-circuits back to the basic biology of wolves. The bulbus glandis, also called the bulb or knot, is an erectile tissue structure on the penis of canid mammals. During mating, immediately before ejaculation, the tissues swell up to lock or tie the male's penis inside the female.

They're basically locked together until the knot deflates. There's no telling how long that would take. If I go by the size of their cocks and the inflatable ring around the base, that could be quite some time.

No. The word floats up my throat but is never released. A drop of creamy pre-cum drips from the tip and steals my worry as though it were nothing more than a carefree afterthought. The creature inside me rises with ecstatic joy as Rif offers his cock to me. My mouth waters and the haze enters my head. Nothing exists other that the need to taste, feel, suck.

"Alpha." The word is right as it falls from my lips, both a question and a command at the same time.

"Honor me and put your mouth on me, omega. Take whatever you need," Rif rasps.

I'm beyond thought as I grab his heated cock in my hands, needing to use both to hold his heavy weight. His hands fall to his hips, giving me total control over him. I look into his burning black eyes as I lean toward him. My tongue darts out and I lap at the tip. Leather explodes on my tongue. I need more. Much more. I dart forward, sucking the end into my mouth.

A low growl is drawn from the bottom of Rif's chest. "Gods . . ."

My thighs grow wetter, my stomach tenses, and another load of slick gushes out of me. A groan tears from me as I grip Rif's cock and suck hard. My tongue traces the shape of his slit topping the thick mushroom head. His scent is more potent here. I breathe him in, needing his taste, his scent, his skin beneath my touch. I squeeze his shaft, trying to milk his cum out of him.

The urge to swallow him is out of control. I'm nothing but a creature of instinct. I drag my slit over Stef's cock and wallow in the sensations sparking through me.

Hot breath warms my peaked breast before Jet locks his mouth around my nipple. I release Rif's shaft to plow my fingers through his snowy-white strands and hold him to my breast while I go back to suck on Rif. I slide my hips over Stef's erection, grinding against him. My stomach lurches. Rif's cock leaves a burning brand on my palm as Jet sucks my hard nipple and Stef holds me steady over his hips.

Yessss. The creature sibilates her euphoria. She's the sole focus of her alphas, and she rejoices.

This. More of this.

"You're weeping all over us. You love us giving you exactly what you need," Stef says.

Yes. Mine. All mine.

Stef or Jet—I don't know who—rubs my clit. My chest tightens. All I can manage are small sucks of Rif's cock, the drag of my tongue, the tilt of my hips, the arch of my back.

Jet slides his rough tongue across my breast with the perfect amount of abrasion. "Look at you, presenting for your alphas. Simply beautiful."

My world narrows to nothing but the sweet sensation of them on my skin. Rif's shaft. Jet's tongue. Stef's fingers holding me steady. Jet grinds down on my nipple.

Slide. Grind. Suck.

The cramps in my belly build into something too big for me to contain. I shake and a bead of sweat dribbles down my spine. Three sets of hands support me. I tilt my hips in frantic hitches and open my jaw as wide as I can to fit Rif's cock between my lips. I suck and grind and sweat and shake.

My eyes fly wide open on a ragged scream as an overwhelming storm crashes through me. Rif threads his fingers through my hair and stuffs his thumb between his cock and my teeth. His shaft throbs and cum splashes into my mouth. He holds my head steady, not letting me move away as he forces his cock past my lips. I can't breathe, but that's a secondary concern to the ambrosia in my mouth.

Stars burst behind my eyes. My pussy throbs. My breasts are tender, and still I drink Rif's essence down. It pools in my belly, mixing with my slick and Stef's and Jet's releases.

Rif releases me and I fall back on top of Stef. Heat splashes on my back as Jet ejaculates over me. Hands rub his essence up my spine and over my shoulders. Stef scoops more of the mess between us and coats my hips, my thighs, my backside. Fingers glide over my rosebud, pushing the liquid inside me. Sparks trail up my spine as a large finger probes me before sliding away. Jet hands join in, rubbing their cum into my skin until it's all gone.

They're in my skin. In my stomach. They lie next to me. I'm in a boneless state and can't move off Stef. His arms band around my back, and Rif and Jet throw their arms around me and weigh me down. I'm a puddle of sated exhaustion. Stef eases my head to his chest over his beating heart.

Their bodies are a deadweight on me, heavy limbs weighing me down. I should feel stifled, but I don't. I'm protected. Comforted.

"Good omega. You've done very well." Rif kisses my temple. His lips twist in a smile as he rests on the pillow next to my face.

The thing in me preens while that rationalizing human part of me recoils in horror. They're not listening to me. They're taking away my autonomy, leaving me without choice. I meant what I said; I don't just want to go home. I *need* to go home. If I don't, I'll be cannibalized by the creature growing stronger inside me with each passing second.

Soon I'll be a husk driven by a biological need that will overpower me until there's no will left inside. I'll be a slave to these aliens and my own sexual urges.

Think, Adele. Think!

I dig my claws into the functioning part of my mind, clearer now that they have satisfied the creature through her orgasms, and work my way past the hazy glow, past the need to sink into sated oblivion that makes my eyelids heavy. I'm a scientist. A woman who works her days away for a cure for cancer. I won't let my sacrifices be for nothing. *I can't.*

I dive into my scientific mind. The familiar thought patterns come back to me, cutting through the haze into clarity. This is what I'm used to, having a clear head without the chaos of emotions taking me over, making me want and do things I have no right to do.

There're two obvious species here. The alphas belong to a medieval culture, dictating how the majority of beings live, with no signs of natural progression, while the other is extremely technologically advanced. It's safe to assume that, like me, they've come here from a different planet. However, there are more of them than just one being, so they must have had a way of getting here other than a freak accident. If they have the technology to get here, they must also have the means to escape.

If this heat hits, they'll bond me—*breed* me—and I'll never get away.

I must find my way back to Earth, by whatever means, before I lose myself forever.

Chapter Nine

Jaetvard

I ring for a servant and order some food for our omega. She'll be hungry when she wakes. Svala, the female beta servant, tries to see past my shoulder when I open the door. I lift my lip and let the growl simmer from my chest. The beta gasps and drops into a quick curtsy. Her cheeks flame when she realizes she's overstepped. "My apologies, my lord."

She clasps her hands and drops her gaze to the ground. It helps appease my flare of anger even when I understand her curiosity. The beta's small black horns, no more than nubbins, peak from her neatly braided dark hair. This female is a good servant and isn't known to cause trouble, so I force myself to calm.

I'll let her have this mistake once. Our omega is a wonder, and the servant's curiosity is to be expected. Word has spread and I expect our people to have many questions about her. We haven't been available to our people since the omega's arrival, and I'm on edge. It's because our omega hasn't slipped into full heat. Her body is stuck in pre-heat and is causing her discomfort, which will only get worse the harder she resists.

"Our omega will wake soon. Have breakfast delivered to this room," I say.

The beta lifts her face, nods quickly, and scurries away along the hallway, her long skirts swishing around her ankles as she disappears down the stairs. The alpha guards I've appointed stand sentinel along the corridor.

"Warlord." Lodin, my Captain of the Guards and a lower alpha, steps from his position against the wall. He wears the black furs of the sevani on his shoulders and the lethal teeth of the fanged animal native to the fires around his neck. The four largest incisors nestle between the flat planes of his pecs. Taking the life of a sevani takes courage and skill. The vicious creatures roam Rjúkaland and account for many lives taken from those who leave the safety of the palisade. They need to be culled regularly to keep the population safe from attack, even in our stronghold.

"Speak," I say.

"D'Kali asked me to let him know when the omega has awoken," Lodin says. His eyes remain on my face and don't stray over my shoulder to the temptation of the omega, to his credit. As an alpha, he would want an omega of his own too. He's a strong alpha and loyal to our pack—which is why I appointed him guard duty over my omega—but still no match for me.

"When did he ask that of you?" Anything concerning the omega should come directly to me and not my guards, no matter how distinguished they may be. D'Kali knows this. And so does Lodin, as he didn't let D'Kali disturb us. It makes little sense that D'Kali would want to be notified, but the Ulgix has taken great pains to keep track of her.

"He came during the night. I sent him away when he would have disturbed you, warlord," Lodin says. His fangs peek beneath his upper lip, evidence he's also concerned by the uncharacteristic actions of the Ulgix.

I nod. "I'll personally let D'Kali know about the omega. If he asks anything of you again, refer to me or my bond brothers straight away."

"As you wish," Lodin says.

I leave him guarding Rif's suite and close the door. Rif sits on the bed while Stef stays wrapped around the omega. Her pale form is tiny compared to his. Her pink-tipped breasts peek from the bedsheets to tease me, and her pale hair is a tangled mess haloed around her head. Stef gently traces her arm and tucks her fine hair off her forehead. She stirs, curling into his touch, but doesn't wake. The little line between the sleek brows smooths as she finds her place nestled against him. It's such a sweet, tender scene that makes my heart wrench all the more because I never thought to have this.

"She knows who she belongs to when she's asleep," Stef whispers.

"If only she was so relaxed awake," Rif says. Worry is etched into tight lines on his face.

"She's a different species from us. Human, she said. Their ways would be different from ours, although an omega should be an omega no matter where she comes from," Stef says.

"She's scared of her nature, locking herself in pre-heat because she denies herself. She'll wear herself out if she doesn't fall into full heat. She should know not to be afraid of her alphas. We exist for her. What have the alphas on her planet done to make her so distrustful?" Rif says.

"It's as though she's rejecting being an omega," I say. I rub my chest where my heart throbs. We've done all we can, and we'll continue to do all we can to help our omega, but there hasn't been an omega born for two decades that we know of. I only know how to treat an omega through my childhood eyes when I saw how my fathers tended to my mother.

"More like she doesn't know how to be one," Rif muses. He cups her ankle, fulfilling the need to touch her, and I yearn to do the same. I'll wake her if I do that, and she needs her sleep. "I've never seen an omega reject her nature before."

"We should ask D'Kali about her species. See if he can shed some light," Stef says, although he doesn't sound confident.

I tell them what Lodin told me. "The omega doesn't trust D'Kali. Nor the serum he injected her with."

"D'Kali has always been our advisor. He's trusted," Rif says. "He aided us in ruling Rjúkaland when my parents died."

"You were young when they perished," I say. I lean against the door, folding my arms over my chest. The Death has consumed our world, the threat always imminent.

Rif's omega mother and alpha fathers died when he was but five years of age. D'Kali and he have always been close. And why should he not trust D'Kali? The Ulgix is a father figure to our most powerful alpha. The Ulgix are long-lived. D'Kali was one of the original Ulgix to come to our aid six generations ago when the disease first struck Amadon before the Solice War. Rif hasn't known D'Kali as anything other than our advisor—nor his fathers or grandparents. D'Kali's support goes back six generations.

"Perhaps he's worried, hoping she doesn't contract The Death. He knows what she means to us," Rif says. "However, our omega trusts us. If she doesn't want any serum or D'Kali to come close to her, then we won't let him."

"We'll protect her from The Death. She won't go anywhere without one of us," I say. If we monitor her every moment, we'll keep her safe.

"During her heat, she won't want to leave the safety of her nest," Stef says.

I frown, looking at the bedding, at the flat sheets she lies on and the pillows on the floor, at the waterfall of blankets from the mattress we've shoved aside when we lay with her, and I feel like the lowest alpha. "She hasn't attempted to make a nest. No wonder she hasn't slipped into heat. She has no nest. Nothing to invite us into!"

I've forgotten the most fundamental aspect of omegas and their heats. I remember my mother's nest, and it was a thing of beauty. Piles of the softest materials, smooth sheets, and soft pillows, lined with the furs of the sevani my fathers hunted for her.

Rif curses and rises to his full height. His claws extend and scrape a bloody welt along his thigh. "I've been so wound up in finding her, it didn't enter my head. She needs nesting materials. I have nothing good enough for her."

"We didn't think of it either. Don't blame yourself, brother," I say. I understand Rif's reaction. We all should have known if we were thinking straight. The joy at finding our omega and the shock of her state when Rif plucked her from the healing fires consumed us all. We've yet to understand how she came to be there from her home planet.

"If she's rejecting her omega biology, it would make sense she'd reject nesting," I say.

A knock taps the door loud enough to make the omega stir, blinking her beautiful blue eyes open. Her plush lips part and she yawns wide enough to crack her jaw. I can't pull my gaze from her. She's adorable waking up, with pink-tinged cheeks and her skin glowing with a rosy sheen. Until full awareness returns.

Her eyes focus into hard, shocked points. She gasps, clutches the sheet, and draws it over her delectable breasts. That's another anomaly. An omega knows never to hide her form from her alphas. She should revel in their attention. Be needy for her alphas' ministrations and compliant as she wakes. We'd welcome her well into a new day.

She notices Stef behind her. My heart tumbles into the pit of my stomach at her first reaction to scramble away from him. He reaches for her and she curls into a ball at the edge of the sleeping platform.

The knock comes again and I detect Svala's light breathing behind the door. I open the door, only because she has food for the omega. I take the tray from her, close the door behind me, and place it at the end of the bed. "Come and break your fast, omega. You need to eat."

Her gaze darts to the open doors and the wide balcony beyond where we take flight on our blazing savimites. I think she wants to see the village below until her eyes lock behind me. She bites her pillowed bottom lip and seeks every door of Rif's rooms, no doubt looking for a way of escape. She's lovely and also intelligent. I shift, hoping she doesn't notice the growing bulge between my thighs. I want her to see how greatly she affects me, but not when she's clearly still on edge.

Tending her through her heat spike should have softened her, and it's clear she's issuing a challenge, demanding her alphas show how well they'll care for her. Fight for her. It's good because my bond brothers are always up for a challenge, especially one as important as her. This female from another planet is an omega worthy of her warlord alphas. She won't be an easy conquest, and the win will be all the sweeter for it.

"Guards are posted outside these rooms," I inform her.

Her striking gaze lands on me. "So you're trapping me here." My cock swells at her husky voice.

"They're for your safety," Rif says. "No one can get in or out without us knowing."

"How many guards?" she asks.

I see through her question instantly. "Too many for you to fight off on your own. We have food for you. What would you like first? I shall feed you." I kneel on the floor, and while she's on the sleeping platform, the action brings us eye to eye. She's such a tiny thing. Dainty and delicate. I'd contain the whole alpha contingent to guard her doors if I could.

Her eyes drop to the tray as though she sees it for the first time. Svala has done an excellent job. There's a selection of delicacies and a steaming container of caffa. The omega's nose twitches. My lips jerk with the curiosity she can't hide. "Is that coffee?"

This coffee must be a delicacy in her world. I pour some of the deep brown liquid into a heat-protected container. "It's caffa. Many enjoy it here."

My heart leaps when she takes the container from me and sips the liquid. I watch her pink lips form around the rim of the container and taste. Her eyelids flutter closed. "It tastes like coffee. Thank God."

"Now eat, omega. You need the sustenance food provides, not just caffa," Rif says.

Her shoulders stiffen and her eyes flash. I make a note to tell my bond brothers our omega doesn't like direct orders. She has never shown us her submissive side. Omegas are well known to be submissive. Perhaps this is another trait of omegas from her planet.

"Please eat," I say, to soften Rif's command.

"Adele," she says.

I don't miss Rif's eyes flaring, but I ignore him. I pick up a piece of sweet pastry and hold it to her lips. "This is sweet citron. It pairs well with the caffa."

She hesitates and I wait, hand poised with the pastry between my fingers. Slowly she reaches for the treat and I take back my hand. She stares at me, a faint line forming between her brows. "It's an alpha's pleasure to feed their omega."

The flash in her eyes makes me smile. I like this fiery version of her. It hooks something inside me and draws me even closer to her. "I'm not an omega. My name is Adele."

The words are pushed between her blunt white teeth. Just as well the pastry is soft, unlike the meat of the coyicit, the large herbivores we breed for food and their shaggy fur. Off the bone, the strongest fangs are needed to rip it apart. Her teeth will not be strong enough.

"Someone who smells like an omega, feels like an omega, looks like an omega, *is* an omega," Rif says. His voice has taken on a growl. Her arms fold over her chest but fail to hide her nipples beading to tent the thin sheet she's covered herself with. In this regard, her response to her alpha is all omega.

I touch the pastry to her lips. She needs to eat, despite the argument Rif wants to find himself in. I know she's hungry if the growling from her stomach is any indication. The tip of her tongue darts out to lick the smear of ground sweetener the tidbit is dusted in.

I see the moment she decides the pastry is delicious. She reaches for it with her hand, and again I pull it away from her. Her eyes spark with blue fire as they dart from it and back to me. My cock throbs, and tingles race through my system. I'm intrigued to see what she'll do next. If she'll let me feed her or how much fight she'll put up. I'll be satisfied either way.

My lips curve because she should know she'll never win this game. I keep that to myself, because I will not see her without sustenance. If she decides she wants to fight, I'm not without ways to bend this creature to my ways.

First I'll kiss her. I'll tweak her nipples until they're distended and a perfect blend of pink and red. I'll chase the flush that will run from her breasts to her neck with my fangs until I reach her dainty earlobe. When I sucked it last night, her flawless skin broke out in tiny bumps that made her shiver. If that doesn't work, then I'll . . .

Stef clears his throat. "You want her to eat that now?"

I see the pastry has crumbled in my fingers and is in pieces on the sheets. The omega's hand darts out to snag another item of food off the tray. "Uh-uh, omega. Feeding you is my privilege."

"Do I get to eat, or do I have to watch you crush everything?" she says.

Her lips turn up and her face lights. It's a flicker, but it's there. I pick up another item and hold it against her lips. Her shoulders droop and a sigh escapes her. My blood sings when she leans in and takes the item from my fingers with a dainty swipe of her lips and tongue.

Now it's my turn to shiver when her lips graze my fingertips. I shift to alleviate the pressure of my hard cock, but I won't give up my position feeding her. Rif and Stef will have to wait their turn.

"Oh!" She holds her hand to her mouth as she chews, thoughtful for a moment. "It tastes like a croissant."

A rumble emits from Stef's chest. His complete attention is trained on her. His body is tense; he barely holds himself together as he watches her eat.

The next bite she takes from me is easier for her. She barely hesitates before leaning to take the food from my hand. Her tongue brushes my thumb. Possession boils in my blood. It's my right, my need, my instinct for her to feed from my hand. This is how she'll take every meal from us from now on.

"Give her the hizil cake next," Rif says. They're both as enthralled as I am, watching her reactions and learning what she likes and what isn't to her taste. I note the possessive gleam on their faces. I'll have a fight on my hands to feed her the next meal.

Her gaze tracks the morsel in my hand and she's about to take it from me when her eyes shutter. She gasps and pulls away so quickly her back slams into the wall. "Oh my God. I was so hungry I forgot."

"You've hardly touched anything," Stef says.

It's true. She's only eaten a few bites of this meal. She's barely eaten anything since Rif brought her to us. The way an omega should meet her alphas has been a disaster. I can't blame her for being wary, but it doesn't change the function of her biology. "Your heat will be hard on your body. You need to build up your energy," I say.

Her brows droop over her perfect eyes, and her plush lips thin. Her cheeks blaze as a pink blush rises from her neck. Her chest heaves. "Stop saying things like that. *Omega . . . Heat . . . Breed . . .* There's mercury in my blood. Who knows what else I may ingest here that will eventually kill me?" She pins me with icy eyes. "I don't come from here. I'm not one of you. My body isn't made for this planet. If I don't get home, it's only a matter of time before it will kill me."

The golden beads embedded into Rif's locs clatter as they move across his back. His temper blazes as hot and fast as the cleansing fires. Our omega clenches the sheets tightly in her little grip, but she doesn't back down.

"Omega . . ." Rif starts, but a pounding at the door stops him.

He flies off the bed and yanks open the door to reveal Lodin snapping to attention, his gaze trained on his warlord. He's out of breath, jaw tight. "Warlord, your attention is required at the mines. There's been an accident."

Chapter Ten

Adele

Rif's dark head jerks over his shoulder to stare at the other two aliens. Stef rises from the bed while Jet moves closer to me. The tray of food is forgotten, as is my outburst, when the alphas act. Rif strides to the balcony, cups his face, and utters a booming sound—a cross between a click and a bark—that echoes into the sky.

He whirls inside, his black eyes raking over me. "We're not leaving the omega here."

My fingers cramp from how tightly I hold the sheet against my pounding heart. I scrunch my body into a ball, willing myself to be invisible and hoping this is all a bad dream, but unfortunately the logical part of my mind functions just fine. The smooth sheet doesn't feel right. The air is too hot. Sweat drips down my back and the light is too bright.

"I'm naked," I squeak.

Jet snatches a bunch of material from the floor. "She'll wear my shirt."

He draws the sheet from my body. Of course, no matter how hard I clutch the sheet, I'm no match for their strength. The sheet drops off me and the next moment he's wrangling my arms and pulling the shirt over my body. He puts his hands beneath my arms and, without any effort, sets me on my feet and tugs down the shirt. The hem falls to below my knees and fits like a bag. I tug the collar to my nose and fill my lungs with sandalwood. The scent acts like an instant dose of Xanax. He makes a sound and I lift my gaze to his face to see a satisfied, sexy smirk cross his lips.

Stef clicks his tongue. He rifles through his clothing and comes to me with a band of leather. He winds it twice around my waist before buckling it. I recognize the strap as one he wears around his chest. Rif picks me up and sits on the bed, with me in his lap.

"What are you doing?" I say.

"Dressing you," Rif says.

I catch a brief look at the demon standing at the door while Jet kneels at my feet and slips a boot onto my foot before my attention snaps down. My foot swims in it. "Too big," he mutters.

"Use this." Stef hands Jet a strip of leather and a thin strap. In seconds, Jet has wrapped one foot and picked up the other one.

"I don't like it. It's not comfortable," I say. The fur-lined leather they've wrapped my foot in is somehow wrong. I can barely stand to feel it against my skin. As vulnerable as I was naked under the sheet, it was preferable to the scratchy shirt and constrictive wrap.

"It won't be for long, omega. We'll be done as fast as we can and soon you'll be comfortable and naked in our bed again, but we can't leave you here unprotected," Rif grunts.

My skin prickles. I'm grateful for the shirt, for any clothing at all, but I hate it at the same time. It tightens around me. I swipe at the sleeve and roll my shoulders, trying to get comfortable, but it's impossible.

Rif kisses my temple. My head tilts of its own accord and he runs his nose along my neck, dragging in air. "Your scent is blooming and we've neglected your nesting. When we get back, we'll help you source the right materials."

"Nesting?" Another swarm of questions bombards me, and again they don't provide me with any satisfying answers. At least none that don't make dread unfurl.

Rif stands and takes my hand. "Are you ready to ride Torbjorn again?"

He tugs me to the balcony where three magnificent creatures burn. Colorful flames rise from their bodies, drifting in languid rivers of reds, oranges, and yellows. Massive wings are tucked close to their sides. They resemble horses, but are twice as big. Their hooves strike the stone, sending sparks fluttering upward.

The terror of being held captive in Rif's arms as he scooped me from being burned alive makes my heels dig into the floor. "I'm not getting on that thing again."

Rif simply wraps me in his massive arms. "Torbjorn won't hurt you. You know that. He's a gentle creature, especially with females I care about immensely."

I'm so caught in his words—*care about immensely*—that I'm only half aware he's mounting the flaming devil horse with me in his arms. No one has ever cared immensely about me. He settles me in front of him. My legs splay across the creature's back. Rif bands a massive arm about my waist and holds me in a crushing grip. He's all carved muscle at my back and enormous thighs framing mine. My skin is pale and stark against his deep crimson. His body is three times as bulked compared to me, but then I stop wondering about our size difference as flames dance about my skin.

They don't burn me as they change to a flurry of pinks and purples for a few seconds before they return to oranges and reds. The creature tosses its head, turning so that its bulging eyes gaze back at me.

I reach out and tentatively pat its neck. The hair is fine and soft beneath my palm, and I can't help smoothing my hand over its neck. I'd be in heaven if this was around my body; it's so soft against my skin. The horse-creature whinnies, and the sound is similar to a cat's purr.

"He likes you." Rif leans down to speak in my ear. His voice is low and although he hasn't said anything charged, I break out with a shiver.

His arm tightens and is the only indication he's aware of my physical reaction to him. And I do react to him. To all of them. The creature hijacks my body; she always simmers below the surface, aware and ready to take me over if I'm not vigilant.

Rif takes the reins in his large hands. Muscles play beneath his forearm as he contains Torbjorn. The horse stamps and rocks under us. Stef and Jet have mounted their horses. Their hooves clatter like gunshots.

"Take as many warriors as you can find and meet us there. Tell D'Kali to bring his team," Rif calls to Lodin. He gives Rif a sharp nod and disappears from the doorway. I didn't see the other demons behind him, but a stream of them flow past the open doorway.

"Yah!" Rif booms and nudges his heels into Torbjorn's sides.

I squeal, my nails digging into Rif's forearms as the horse pumps its powerful wings and lifts from the balcony. We rise and turn toward a series of blackened volcanoes along the horizon. Plumes of gray climb from the tips, sending smoke to cloud the sky, and I know I'm on borrowed time. Carbon dioxide, sulfur dioxide, hydrogen sulfide, and hydrogen halides are contained in the smoke. If the mercury doesn't kill me, the toxic volcano fumes will.

I take in the panorama of twisting streets and hundreds of thatched rooftops dotting the village beneath me. People mill within the streets and look up as we fly overhead. We pass over the palisade, with its immense wooden poles. Each pole is meters round and sharpened to a fine point. Aliens armed with swords patrol the inner walkway.

"I wonder how many people live here," I murmur to myself. The village looks to be full, but the blackened fields beyond the palisade are nothing but charred earth.

Smoke rises from blackened tufts. The ground is barren and black and empty. The dead ground is broken with cracks of steaming red as molten rock moves within. A rumble steals my attention and water sprays into the sky, turning to steam before it can reach the earth. The surface is far too hot for a human to survive, given the landmarks. It's hot, and yet my skin is not cooking on my body.

"Three thousand souls live within the walls of Kjorseyrr," Rif says.

The air beats with the thrust and pull of Torbjorn and the two beasts flying either side of us. Jet's pure white hair streams behind him. Flashes of gold glint in the sunshine. He throws me a wide grin as he rides, his body moving in sync with the beast, two moving as one.

Stef is also as impressive. Flames lick around his thighs, and his long electric-blue fire is striking compared to the warm hues of the horse. His face is a mask of concentration. His cheeks are chiseled slashes, and his mouth is set in a tight line as he keeps half his attention on me and the other on the volcanos fast approaching.

"Three thousand," I repeat. That's a lot, yet empty land stretches from horizon to horizon. I would expect more population density taking in the available land.

"In my grandparents' time, our population was ten times greater. Our stronghold was larger too, of course," Rif says.

"Your population has dropped that significantly in three generations?" I say.

"It's The Death, little omega. What we're desperately protecting you from. It came to our planet six centuries ago and has decimated our population. Our planet was nothing like it is today. There were towering buildings. Technology such as the Ulgix use. There was no need for savimites to ride because we had conveyances that ran on fuel. There was a thriving community of alphas, omegas, and betas. Amadon was so large and strong we led the galaxy with our military," he says.

My breath stutters and my chest turns to concrete. It is hard to comprehend the life he describes when compared to what I currently face. It sounds as if this planet experienced a very slow mass-extinction event. There had to be an event that triggered it.

"Did you say galaxy?" I ask. This society is medieval in style. They have warriors. These demons are warlords and rule through strength alone. His knowledge of a galaxy is a jarring juxtaposition.

"We were a leader of worlds until The Death targeted our omegas." His words are filled with heaviness. "Less and less were born. At first, it wasn't noticeable, but after two hundred years, our population suffered. Without omegas, alphas and omegas aren't born. Betas are too weak to be warriors. Our military became weaker until it dwindled enough for an interplanetary threat that endangered our world. Luckily the Ulgix arrived to help us fight for our freedom," he says.

My head is filled with war. Of an entire race dying out. Of a planet changing and becoming uninhabitable. "Did that cause the earth to char and burn?"

"No, omega. What you see below is natural. Soon our flora will grow and the coyicits will emerge from our land where we'll hunt them and prepare them to feed our people for the year to come," Rif says.

I can't imagine anything could change so drastically. The land below looks charred and dead. The scientist in me switches on, trying to work out how any new life could begin from such a place. There's nothing down there. No sign of green. No movement apart from the occasional geyser spraying into the air.

Now that I'm able to study them, they don't seem as large and powerful as the one that erupted over me when I found myself here. Geysers don't behave that way. They're usually in the same location and erupt on a semi-regular basis, but the geysers here erupt at random. There must be huge volcanic activity beneath the crust . . .

Rif leans to speak in my ear. "I can see your interest has sparked. I'll personally show you the fields. The new life. Our reawakened animals. I'll show you every inch of your new world with the greatest pleasure for however long you want to see it."

I look over my shoulder to study his expression. I don't know how he picked up on my interest, but he has. Surprise shoots through me when I realize he's serious. He's not just saying words or making empty promises. He *wants* to show me. No one has cared enough for that. I've never had anyone so focused on my needs. On . . . me.

I've forged ahead on my own. Anything I've achieved has been through hard work and dedication. I've had to explain the purpose of my goals in minute detail for anyone to understand how I feel or what I desire. Even less who understand why I do what I do. I'm so used to the battle that I look for it wherever I am.

I'm fully aware of another type of battle between us, but that's something different. Something on a whole other level I don't even want to entertain right now. The awareness inside me peeks one eye open, rolls, and stretches. It cares nothing about my wariness and isn't concerned about being what it is and doing what it drives me to do. And that's more unnerving than anything.

Rif flicks the reins and Torbjorn tilts his wings. We fly through the smoke of the volcanoes, and I'm surprised I'm not choking on toxic fumes. I probably shouldn't even be conscious, and yet I am. Everything I think about this planet is upside down.

Or maybe it's me who's changing. Adapting...

"Thankfully the Ulgix came to our rescue despite the seasons changing. The only species to suffer this degenerative disease has been us. They work with us to find a cure and have done for six centuries now. We're grateful they stayed to help us after the Solice War was won, otherwise we'd probably be the slaves of our invaders," he says.

A plume of a different kind rises into the air. Black dust particles scatter in the breeze and filter back down to the earth from the black cloud it makes. Rif barks a sound that snaps Torbjorn into action. We hurtle to the ground. My stomach rolls at our speed. We drop at an impossible pace until Torbjorn's wings snap like a sail. His hooves slam onto the ground, but I barely feel the impact.

Then I'm not thinking of the strange horse made of flames in favor of the devastation in front of me. Rif leaps from Torbjorn, leaving me perched on his back. Stef and Jet land next to me. With practiced ease, they dismount. Dirt sprays beneath their feet.

We're at the base of the volcano. Several dark holes line the vast side. Steel tracks line the ground, leading to several large conveyances. Hundreds of full carts have come to a stop on the track, each filled to the brim with chunks of black stone. This is a very complex mine site. Successful too, if the full carts and enormous piles of crushed rock are any indication. This is another anomaly for the medieval society I've fallen into.

"Protect her," Rif yells. Stef and Jet's horses surround me. Torbjorn's wings fold around my legs and waist. I can't move and there's no way I will unless they release me.

"We'll be back, omega. Our savimites will protect you with their lives. They understand how precious you are," Rif says.

The ground shakes as more alpha demons land on the ground. The savimites toss their heads and bark as the warriors jump from their backs and rush away.

These creatures must be intelligent because they understood Rif's command, but then my three alphas run off. I don't call them back. I can't because the scene before me is chaos. Smaller Amadonians—betas, I guess—dart toward a large hole in the ground where black dirt and steam continue to rise. They're frantic as they dig, but their efforts appear largely futile.

They part to let the larger alphas through. I can see why the alphas are at the top of their society. They're head and shoulders above the betas. They're more muscular. Their horns are bigger and the sheer weight of their presence is undeniable. Betas are weaker, thinner, and more subservient, bowing and acting immediately upon any alpha command.

The alphas take hand tools. I don't think the tools will be any match for the dirt blocking the mine entrance, but I'm wrong, and they plow through. Rif, Stef, and Jet are by far the strongest. The muscles in their shoulders tense. Their faces set in grim lines of determination. They're ... magnificent. I'm embarrassed to find my core heating and liquid seeping between my thighs.

Several beta faces turn my way, their nostrils twitching. I notice the sweet scent wafting around me, like a cloud of arousal. I shouldn't be feeling this way. Not with so obvious a tragedy right in front of me. Torbjorn stamps his feet and shifts.

A cry goes up as my alphas disappear into the hole they made. Every muscle in my body locks to see them vanish behind the wall of rubble. Other alphas follow them inside. There's no telling how unstable it is behind the collapse. Anything could happen to them.

I can't look away until they reappear. They're holding bodies, one under each arm. They gently lay the beings on the ground and dash back into the hole. One by one, the demons reappear until there's about twenty unconscious betas they've saved. They're not moving and I don't understand why no one is offering medical help until a flash of steel catches my attention.

The reptile beings shoot through the sky toward us. They stand on something large, flat, and silver, like a HoverDisc. The technology is jarring, as though it doesn't belong here. D'Kali clutches a waist-high handlebar attached to the HoverDisc and leads them toward us. His white robes flutter around his legs as he lands. His eyes never leave me. I wrap my fingers in Torbjorn's flaming mane, happy to have the creature beneath me.

The reptiles—the Ulgix—land and walk to the betas. There's something about the way they triage that rubs me the wrong way. There's no urgency. No care. I recognize the look because it's the same way I look at the cells I'm researching. These beings are specimens to the Ulgix. Nothing more than that.

My alphas stand back, chests heaving and muscles shining with their exertions, and let the Ulgix sort through the betas. D'Kali strides between them, offering commands while looking over the bodies. He kneels over the betas and waves a scanning device over them. They take the beings D'Kali points at to the discs and fly away. After they leave, there are about five betas left on the ground. They're not dead because I can see them breathing.

Panic makes my hands tremble as the Ulgix disappear back to the stronghold. They've left some betas behind. I try to get off Torbjorn's back, but it's impossible. Stef strides over to me. I'm not surprised he's noticed my growing alarm.

"Get me down, Stef," I say.

He looks at me with darkened eyes. His shoulders droop and I can sense his sadness as well as he senses my panic. "There's nothing to be done, omega. These betas won't survive."

"How do you know?" I cry.

"The Ulgix have tested," he says.

I point to the closest male who is struggling to breathe. "His chest is caved in. He's probably got a punctured lung. Call them back to get him. It's not too late." Their technology is far superior to Earth's. I know they'll have a way to help him.

I try to push Torbjorn's wings away, but I get nowhere. The fire horse isn't letting me off. Stef slowly shakes his head and a pit opens in my stomach. Rif and Jet join us. Rif's brows are slashes over his eyes and tense lines appear around Jet's mouth.

"There's nothing you can do, omega," Rif says.

The betas finally surround the beings on the ground, kneeling next to them and uttering soft words. Almost as if they're waiting for them . . . to die. "It's not too late. I can help . . . I can do *something*."

A wail rises from a group surrounding one of the betas. My heart races as I know another life is lost. It's happening so fast. They're fading before my eyes. My life's work is about saving lives and I'm stuck here on this horse, not able to do a damn thing.

"You have to calm yourself, omega. Being upset isn't good for your health," Jet says. His horse lets him through, and he curves his hands over my thigh.

"Upset? My *health*? Let me down. Let me look at them. Why aren't you listening to me?" I say.

A wail rises, and another. Before I can draw three more breaths, the betas have died. The creature inside me shoots to life. Her wail becomes mine. A strange sound fills my ears. A sound so sorrowful I can barely believe it exists. My chest feels empty even though I'm dragging in breath after breath, and I can't get enough oxygen. I'm dizzy. Black edges my vision when I realize it's me making that sound.

Cedar fills my lungs as sure hands lift me off Torbjorn. Stef positions me so I'm straddling him atop his horse. Wind whips my hair as we rise and I bury my nose in his chest, breathe him in, taking comfort in his scent, his body, his presence, at the same time hating that I do that. I clench his clothing and wind my legs around his waist, trying to make sense of what I just witnessed.

Sadness greater than I've ever felt overcomes me, but there's also anger. I might not know a lot about this world, but I understand enough. I didn't know these betas, but the awareness in me doesn't care. Those males were sorted like commodities by the reptile race. Their lives held no value. Judged on a whim who will live or die by a being I don't trust—and neither does the awareness inside me. There's something about D'Kali and the others that fills me with boundless hatred.

My anger takes on another facet. It's multi-sided with sharpened edges, brought alive with my new awareness. My alphas didn't listen to me. The Ulgix didn't listen to me. They think I'm a commodity, like those betas.

They've all made a grave mistake.

Chapter Eleven

Adele

We're in a cathedral made from shining black stone, and I stand on a lip of stone surrounded by my—*the*—alphas. I shuffle on the cool stone beneath my feet, taking everything in. Smooth columns connected by flying buttresses have been carved to create a masterpiece from a cave set in one of the volcanoes. From the outside the cave was merely a black hole, but inside is a thing of beauty.

I crane back my head. The ceiling expands way overhead. Each section of the stone is decorated; nothing is left plain or untouched. Hidden lights cleverly illuminate the walls and enhance the spectacular space and throw light to the smooth patchwork of stone below as well as on the sunken relief along the walls. The design encompasses the wall from one side of the entrance to the other, intricate and flawless.

My eyes draw along the frieze that tells a story of battles. Of demons riding flaming horses. Of creatures coming from the clouds to save a population. This world was once an advanced civilization, at such odds with the simple life they live now. *Simple on the outside*, I correct myself. They've known technology. *Know* technology. The reptiles use it beneath their noses, but the natives of the planet don't use it themselves.

Sounds of crying draw my attention back to the large crowd of demons/Amadonians below us. They fill the large floor space, possibly every person from the stronghold. A jagged river of red glowing lava divides the grand floor. The molten rock moves in a sluggish meander beneath the crack in the smooth black floor. Steam rises and swirls upward.

Five black pods with sharply pointed ends line the river and contain the bodies of the betas who died in the mine collapse. They're wrapped in reams of white cloth, leaving their crimson faces visible. Families kneel next to each pod, comforting one another. The mood is somber and contained, heaviness pressing around me. My heart aches for the dead and for the families who've lost loved ones.

A song sweeps through the crowd. Haunting and beautiful, it fills the cavern and echoes around us. The deep basses of the males complement the lighter voices of the fewer females. It's a song of loss and heartbreak, of unending sadness and the type of grief that will never pass. The melody sweeps me away with its beauty.

I close my eyes and clear my head of my parents' funeral. One for my mother when I was young, and the other for my father when I understood what loss was. As though they can sense my mood, the alphas shift around me. Jet puts his arms around me and moves me against his tree-trunk torso. He nuzzles my temple and presses a soft kiss there. I lean into him, thankful for the comfort before I catch myself and pull away. Concentrating on the masses below helps center me.

None of the reptiles are here, and there's no sign of D'Kali. Most of the people are clearly betas. The differences in sheer body mass are obvious now that I see them in a large group like this. I pick out a few alphas, but none are as large as the warlords framing me. There are females, but I sense they're also beta. The creature in me that has become alarmingly stronger during these past two days settles when she sees there are no rivals among them, and my sweet apple-blossom scent perfumes around me for no reason.

There are no omegas, although what they may look like, I have no idea. Perhaps they are the smaller females the sculpture depicts. I'd thought at first they may have been children, but I see them always surrounded by a pack of much larger alphas. The omegas in the sculpture are fully mature. They have curves and breasts, and are often nurturing a baby at their breast or have young children clinging to their skirts. The alphas surround the females like bodyguards. They look fierce, horns locking, swords drawn, claws slashing omega-less packs who threaten their families.

It's feral and brutal. I shift on my feet, uncomfortable with the attention I'm garnering from this vantage point. A few betas and most of the alphas throw glances up at us. Their nostrils flare. I'm sure they can smell the scent my body throws off. It's getting stronger. More lush. It's particularly strong when cramps steal my breath and wetness seeps from me. Slick. It's an apt name.

The fluid is thick and fragrant. It's not a normal secretion, and when it gushes from me, my needs are overwhelming. I'm wanton. I don't care if I abandon myself to them. I want to drop to my hands and knees and bury my face in the mattress, my ass in the air, pussy throbbing and begging to be filled.

I manage to stop myself every time it happens, but it's getting harder. I'm assailed with intense urges. I almost jumped out of my skin with joy when Stef brought in armfuls of soft material and furs, and I lost myself stroking the material while they looked indulgently on. Waiting for something unnamed. When I came back to my senses, I left the blankets in a heap in the corner of the room, not daring to walk close to it ever since.

I feel the alphas below searching for me. This is the first time I'm on display like this. Their lingering gazes steal over me, most probably noting my human differences. There's more when I study them just as closely. Certainly curiosity. Awe, and . . . it's the longing that makes my gaze slide to Rif standing so close to me that his arm grazes mine.

During the past two days the cramping has gotten worse. Heat breaks through me, burning me up from the inside and pouring out in beads of sweat over my body. I can't eat. I barely drink. I'm weakened, but I'm not giving in to the creature inside me that demands to break free. I keep her locked deep inside behind mental bars of steel.

I know if she breaks out, I'll lack the will to find a way back home. So I stuff her back down whenever she rears up. It's a standoff because I'm determined I'll get back to Earth and she's determined to turn me into a slick-producing breeder.

I've formed a shaky plan that relies on somehow getting away from the alphas. I've been waiting for them to leave me alone, but they don't take their eyes off me. Not for an instant. At least one of them is with me all the time. I'm grateful and I'm not. Their touch alleviates the twisting lava in my stomach, but I can't go far from them without the fire igniting.

And their touches . . . so gentle. Careful. They're concerned for me. Watching and waiting for the thing in me to bloom beyond my control. As the days pass, they're becoming more worried. I catch their nervous looks. The conversations they stop when I'm near.

I've told them I want to go home so many times I can't count them. I've pleaded. I've cried. They soothe me with words and caresses and kisses that drug my system and leave me clinging to my sanity with willpower alone. Every time it happens I'm a little closer to losing myself.

Despite how upset I am, they don't listen. They keep me wrapped in their delicious scents and their bodies. Their single-minded, hypnotizing, anesthetizing attention. They're going to make me forget who I am. What I strove for. They'll obliterate the sacrifices I've made. The hours of long, back-breaking work I've given. The gift of a cure for cancer that could extend human life and save millions of people.

The alphas flew me here on the back of Torbjorn from the stronghold and across the charcoal fields. They're subdued, obviously caring that they lost people to the mine collapse. I've still yet to know what happened to the people D'Kali took away. Rif tells me they're being cared for, but I don't forget the callous choosing of that day. It's wrong to decide who will live and die without a fight at least, and is yet another thing the alphas aren't listening to me about.

Rif steps forward. His deep voice echoes throughout the cavern. "We give back these bodies to the river of blood that connects our worlds. We thank our planet for these bodies and the souls who were able to inhabit them. We ask that our planet take back the forms from which life flowed and ask that they are returned with the gifts of flesh so that more life may remain abundant on our world."

When he's finished speaking, six people lower the pods into the lava. As the pods drift along the river, another song begins. Goosebumps break over my skin at the haunting tone. Their collective grief surrounds me, filling a hole inside me. The creature awakens and keens, the sounds inside me nearly breaking from my lips.

The pods drift along the lava river. Embers flare around the edges of each pod and flames lick up the sides, enveloping the pods as they slowly sink into the molten flow. It's beautiful and tragic. We watch as the pods disappear. Rif's words hold truth, and I see the meaning of them. The song reaches a peak and silence falls.

Everyone turns to walk from the cathedral, grief etched onto their faces. The loss of a few families affects them all. This disease *has* affected everyone here. They've all lost their forefathers and if what Rif told me about omegas dying off is true, I can see they've also lost more than that.

The reality of their situation sinks in and turns my stomach to sludge. It's no wonder the alphas don't let me go. My body can give their society what it's lost. More omegas. More alphas. I can breed those designations to them. My scent turns sour and my nose twitches. The alphas below look up at me, and this time their gazes are more calculating and leave me cold. My scent has done something to them. They're losing control.

I burrow into Rif, Stef, and Jet and try to hide between their bodies as best I can. The quiet melancholy of the funeral is left behind in place of something darker, more insidious. The creature in me watches from behind my eyes, still for once and aware of the ominous charge in the air.

I look back at the frieze, understanding the story it tells. Alphas fight over their omegas and after decades of this sickness, I'm the only omega in the stronghold to fight over. There are a lot of alphas here and they look as though they would all take what I'm unwilling to give. Every. Single. One.

My blood turns to sleet when I realize what that might mean. These alphas don't have the restrained strength of the warlords, and something is clearly agitating them. They're the alphas who found me in the field when I woke here. Feral with clear, base intentions.

"Come, omega, ride with me." I make no complaint as Jet picks me up as if I'm a child and bundles me against his body. Torbjorn takes to the air. Jet's solid thighs are tense beneath me, and he holds me so tight I can barely move. Rif and Stef fly beside us.

I recognize the alpha who guarded the door, Lodin, right behind us. There are several alphas beside him, flying in formation, dressed in a similar fashion with black pelts over their shoulders and weapons at their hips, but they don't watch me like the others. Their attention is on the alphas flying behind them.

"To my rooms. As fast as we can," Rif barks.

"Hold on to me, omega." Jet flicks the reins and digs his heels into the horse's flanks. We streak through the air with savage pumps of the beast's wings. The ground passes under us in a blur.

Something shifts in the line of alphas behind us. They fan out, matching our pace and bracketing us as the horde behind us follows in a menacing swarm of alpha males riding their flaming horses. I clutch Jet's shirt, press my nose into his chest, and take comfort in his scent. It makes no sense. It won't save me if that horde catches me, but his scent still calms me.

The stronghold is upon us. As soon as we land, Jet leaps from the horse, keeping me bundled in his arms, and bolts inside. He runs to the bathroom, where the healing waters took away the cuts and damage to my body, and sets me on the ground.

"You'll be safe here. We'll make sure they don't get to you," he says.

Rif and Stef grab massive, sharp swords from where they're kept on the walls and dash back to the balcony.

"Why are they like that?" I'm breathless now, panic making my hands shake. The alphas changed. Something set them off as we left. They'd turned from grief-stricken to feral in moments.

"They've turned to their baser instincts and want to claim you," Jet says.

Dread pools a black sludge in the pit of my stomach. I've been locked in this room since I've been here. No one has scented me.

Perhaps that was why the alphas kept me here. There's no way of knowing why those alphas in particular have turned feral.

But if the feral alphas are like this now, then what will happen tomorrow? Will they get worse? They might never go away. I'll never be free. My alphas can only fight for so long. They're outnumbered. I'll always be chained inside. Locked in this room until this miraculous heat takes away my control and my autonomy. I will truly be a breeding vessel and nothing more.

"Claim me?" My voice is as thin as the blood coursing through my veins.

"They'll claim you. Bite you. Bond you. They won't care you're not in heat yet. They're beyond logic now," Jet says.

"How?" I gasp.

Shadows shift over Jet's face. "I don't know. I've never seen this level of feral. This is . . . out of character."

A booming roar and the clatter of hooves pounding on the balcony steal my attention. Rif's and Stef's muscles bulge, and I swear they've grown twice as large. Their biceps tense as they swing swords to fend the alphas away. Flames flicker and wave into the sky off the horses' wings as the alphas keep trying to land, their senseless, blind fury written on their faces. Their eyes blaze a deep red as they streak from the sky like bullets.

"What will they do to me if they get to me?" I ask.

Jet's eyes flatten and his jaw hardens. "They won't get to you, omega. They may try but they'll fail. We fight for what's ours."

He closes the door and I'm left in the room made from solid rock. I run to the door and test it, but it doesn't budge. I hear a lock turn and the doorknob disappears into the door. I'm stuck here. Caged.

If the feral alphas break through and get into this room, I'll have no hope. Panting with lungs too small for my fear, I look for a way out. There's no way I'm waiting here for my impending doom.

A roar shakes the doorframe and something shatters. I hear grunts accompanied by sounds of a fight, then a pain-filled scream.

I'm not waiting here a moment longer. I'm not helpless, and I refuse to give away my autonomy for my safety. I can't expect them to get hurt while trying to protect me.

The water enters the bathing tub from a small opening and drains along a channel at the end of the tub and out of the room. Steam rises from the water, but the air remains clear. There has to be some sort of ventilation. I glance up and see a grill along the top of the wall. A grill large enough for me to slip through.

I stand on the toilet and then step onto the cistern above it, grabbing the grate with both hands. I shriek when something large and heavy slams into the door. The door shakes but stays on its hinges—but for how long? I'm not waiting here to find out.

I rip the grate from the hole, throw it to the ground, then haul myself up using the lip as leverage, forcing my way through. The edge digs into my hips and I scrape some skin, but I don't care. That's nothing in the face of looming mass rape.

I see the hallway outside the shaft on the other side. A tunnel leads directly upward, but there's no way I'll be able to climb straight up. I peer through the grate and finding the hallway clear, punch out the grate with the heels of my hands. It falls to the floor below. I take a moment to make sure no one comes running before I force my way through, tumbling to the ground. Then I pick myself up on shaking legs and run.

Chapter Twelve

Adele

Adrenaline punches through my veins and my feet pound on the wooden boards as I dart along the hallway. I have no idea where I am or who might be around the corner because I've been locked in that damn room for days. I hope no one hears me. Out of the room, I have no hope of protecting myself against the alpha horde if they come for me.

I reach the end of the hallway, flatten my back against the wall, and peek around the corner. Everything inside me prompts me to run, to keep going. I'm a scientist, not a cop or an action hero. Regarding what I should do, I can only go by the occasional action movie I've seen, and that's just stupid and flimsy.

All I know is I can't wait for these feral alphas to destroy me. I dash around the corner into another empty corridor containing a set of stairs. There are no guards here, as I'm sure they're helping fight the alphas on the balcony. Good for me.

I bolt to the stairs and run down them so fast my feet slip on the steps. I catch myself on the banister and keep going. My legs are an uncoordinated mess. My lungs are empty bellows and my blood is liquid panic. I fly down to the first floor and see a double set of decorative doors. High black hinges hold the door to the wooden walls. Two massive metal loops hang at mid-level. I run across the space, hoping those circle things are door handles.

Sweat trickles down my back. I'm coated in sticky heat. I hope my scent doesn't give me away. It seems to be peaking, but I'm going to run as fast as I can. Hopefully it'll be left behind before anyone notices.

I wrench the handles, putting my whole body into action. They're heavy, but I'm fueled by adrenaline. I manage to twist the handle. A heavy metal snap sounds, and one half of the doors cracks open.

My breath catches but I don't waste any time. I peek outside. Above me to my right, the battle rages. Alphas circle the balcony on their winged horses. The sky is alight with curling flames. Cries, grunts, and whinnies resound. I hear a deeper, booming roar that makes the horses scatter, and I know the inhuman sound comes from Rif. The sight is barbaric and terrifying, and the creature inside me screams to run. The fight makes her ill. Something isn't right about it, but both sides of me want to get away. At least in this, we're working in harmony.

Some alphas fall back and fly away from the melee. These males are only slightly bigger than the male betas and have thankfully left the fight. The street below is filled with Amadonians watching above. Several guards dressed in black furs and leather straps holding various weapons hold them back. Everyone looks at the fight overhead. Their attention is diverted, and I take the opportunity to slip out.

Rough gravel crunches under my bare feet, but there is no time or opportunity to snatch boots. I force my attention from my feet and stay in the shadows against the side of the stronghold. A flash of white captures my attention, and I spot an Ulgix reptile peering around the corner of the castle building. It lifts something to its mouth and speaks before darting away unnoticed—apart from me. From where I'm backed against the wall, it didn't see me.

The Ulgix would know where to hide by the look of it, so I follow, dashing along the line of the castle until I reach the corner. I see the tail of the creature's white coat as it disappears, seemingly into the castle wall.

That . . . can't be right.

I jog to where the Ulgix disappeared. There's nothing but a solid wall made from the rock-hard wood the entire village has been built from. It's impossible. The being can't vanish into thin air. I reach and feel along the wall and find a thin, barely-there line.

I whirl around at an enraged roar that shakes the ground beneath my feet. Rif launches himself off the balcony and drops to the ground. Gravel sprays and scatters beneath his feet before he charges toward me.

"Omega!" he yells. His face is a rictus of fury.

My chest squeezes. I'm in the middle of a long wall, with no way to hide. Stef and Jet launch themselves from the balcony after him. They bring the horde of alphas streaming behind them. They plow through alphas as they fall from the sky. Jet slams the flat side of his sword into the stomach of one alpha. His knees buckle and he collapses.

Stef wrenches the clothing of another. The force of his swing sets the male off his feet. He slams into a building and crumples to the ground.

There are only three of my alphas and fifty behind them. They can't fend off the ferals forever. I have nowhere to run except for the door the Ulgix went through. I can't let any of them get to me.

I trace the near-invisible line, pressing along the edge. My hands shake and I'm losing my focus because I'm terrified. Come on, come on, *come on*! The door swings open with a quiet click, and I push through as Rif barrels in after me. I'm thrown forward and lose my footing, but Rif throws his arms about my waist and sweeps me off my feet.

Stef and Jet follow, careering in after us. The roar of the feral alphas thunders around us until Jet slams the door closed. We're surrounded by silence. I don't even hear pounding on the other side, although it's loud inside my head. Blood thuds in my ears and my throat pulses with each thumping heartbeat, but at least the door remains shut. The only barrier keeping those crazed alphas away from me.

"What do you think you're doing?" Stef rounds on me. His electric-blue hair streams around his shoulders. His clothing is torn, and through the tears in his shirt, I see bruises covering his chest. Blood streaks his forearms and drips to the ground. He's wild and ferocious in his anger. The creature within me perks up. She *likes* him this way.

"I ordered you to stay where you were," Jet roars. His white hair is a tangled mess. Blood is a stark crimson on his strands and spatters across his chest.

"Ordered me?" I say, struggling to free myself from Rif's arms. Jet has lit an instant flame to my anger. "Put me down."

"Do you understand what would have happened if one of those alphas got to you?" Rif's arms close around me, threatening to sever me in half.

"Do I understand? *Of course I understand*. There are crazed males, ready to rip me apart. I heard them in the room. They were coming after me, so I did the only thing I could and got out of there."

"We would have kept you safe!" Stef's black eyes gleam in the bright white light of the corridor we find ourselves in. The harsh lighting doesn't do anything to make him look less fearful.

One glimpse of his fangs should have me quaking in terror, but I'm beyond that now. He's angry, but so am I. "I keep telling you, I'm not a woman who waits for others to save me. I'm not of this world. Nor am I one of the prized omegas of your planet. I'm a human and I know how to look after myself. Now. Let. Me. Go!" I yank Rif's immobile arm. I don't care that my palms slip in blood. I'm sick of this planet. Sick of being this omega. Sick of feeling as though I'm burning alive from the inside out.

He sets me on my feet, and I spin and back away, surprised he let me go. I take them in, all three large, ferocious, and looming over me. I was terrified of them at first, but not now. Now I'm just pissed. It's been an emotional day, and it seems the day is not through with me just yet.

I tip my chin and point at their chests. "And stop manhandling me. I have two feet and I'm not a child."

"Omega," Jet begins.

"I have a name. It's Adele. Not omega. I don't belong to you. The women—females—of your planet might have been possessions once, but I'm not. I'm not like you, and no amount of huffing and puffing and pushing me into any mold will help."

"We're only looking out for you," Stef says.

His words temper the fury flowing through me because he does look remorseful and is more than a little blood-soaked. My chest heaves as I speak, the words tumbling from me. "I know, but I look out for me too. I'm not safe here and don't want to be here. Not if I'm going to be locked in a room for the rest of my life. That's no way to live. I refuse to live that way. I will not live that way."

Rif steps toward me, his dark gaze endless. "Their behavior is out of character."

"Not from what that frieze depicted in your cathedral," I say.

Rif closes his eyes momentarily. "That's a religious tale, reminding alphas that their omegas are the most precious things in their life. They should be cherished and protected beyond their own physical safety, no matter the actions of others. It's not like that in reality."

I point to the closed door that, thankfully, has remained sealed. "Then why did they act like that? Jet said they caught my scent. Is that what's driving them insane?"

"An unclaimed omega's scent drives an alpha wild, but never to this extent. Their behavior is unprecedented," Stef says. Jet had said the same.

I put my arms about my belly, suddenly cold. As adrenaline seeps from my system, I'm shaking again. This isn't a civilized society. It may have been at one stage, but it isn't now. Evolutionarily speaking, they had changed and it hadn't taken long. Today wasn't evolution, though.

Today was something else entirely.

"In science, you always look for outliers. Something has caused them to behave like that. There has to be some kind of catalyst. My arrival here and those alphas turning feral can't be a coincidence." I pause, looking at the bright white light and metallic corridor that is such a difference to the black wood and rustic style of their village. The hallway is illuminated to the pinpoint of darkness at the other end.

Unease weaves through me, replacing the terror. "This corridor can't be a coincidence either."

"How did you even know it was here?" Rif says.

"I followed an Ulgix lab assistant. It was watching you fight and then it ran inside here. I followed it to . . . get away," I say.

"You mean to be safe," Jet says. His forehead creases and his eyes are fathomless pools as he stares down at me.

"I . . ." I don't know what to say. "I don't feel unsafe with . . . *you*. It was . . ."

Stef reaches for me. His arm bands around my waist and he slowly draws me toward him. I let him pull me against his larger, harder body and inhale his cedar scent into my lungs, a sigh rippling through me without the screaming creature inside me demanding things I would never give. My body slowly relaxes against his. "You didn't feel safe from the other alphas, but only because deep down, we haven't done the right thing."

My fingers clutch his torn clothing. "I can't go back outside."

"We wouldn't do that to you." Rif clears his throat. "The truth is, we don't know why this corridor is here. If you're talking about outliers, then this is something we can investigate. That is . . . if you want to."

A line forms between Rif's brows. He drops his gaze to the floor before bringing it to our surroundings. The line grows deeper as he studies the walls.

"I'd like to see where the Ulgix I followed went," I say.

Rif's gaze focuses on me. He weighs me up and gives me a short nod. "If I give you a direction, it's to keep you safe, not to take away your decision. My bond brothers and I have trained together since we were younglings. We're used to each other and can read each other's body language faster than speech. We can keep you safer if we know where you are at all times, not left wondering where you might be."

"Okay," I say. I prefer this version of Rif and I won't do or say anything to make him go back to his Neanderthal version.

"We keep our positions around her. Don't let her out of your sight," he says to Jet and Stef.

Maybe I read more into his earlier words than he meant, but it doesn't matter because we move as a team down the corridor toward the shadowed end. It's not lost on me that they're unwittingly helping me to my ultimate goal of trying to get back to Earth.

My footsteps are heavier than the alphas'. My feet slapping on the metal floor echoes against the walls, while they tread lightly despite their enormous size. The end of the tunnel reveals a staircase. Glowing lamps highlight the way as we approach and descend the stairs. Down and down we go. The air grows colder and damp, and I shiver at the difference from the constant heat. It's impossible to know how deep we go, but we finally step onto a solid floor. Within reaching distance is another door. Rif's large hand closes around the handle. My heart races as he cracks it open, and with a long sideways glance at me, he leads the way through.

I slip behind him, and Jet and Stef follow. Rif catches my biceps and he pulls me next to him, flat against the wall, when I would have wandered straight into the massive sleek cavern. I can't quite comprehend what I see. The cavern is so large, I can't see the other side beyond the streamlined spacecraft and the huge vats and cascading waterfalls tumbling from them.

Ulgix walk along pathways overhead, checking items off clipboards they hold. Plastic coverings protect them from the waterfalls' spray. The rumbling sound of crashing water booms around me from five waterfalls tumbling into a frothing catchment area before disappearing through a giant grate along a rocky wall.

That isn't the only thing that catches my attention. Not why there are giant waterfalls under the stronghold. Or even why the Ulgix monitor the water. Or how there are spacecraft in a section behind the waterfalls. No, it's the large filters the water is forced to pass through, the complex array of lights on the consoles surrounding the system, and what they're monitoring.

A silver pipe overhead runs the length of the consoles and drips a liquid into the water. The water sweeps away silver drops that are injected at regular intervals into the stream. The churning waters are the perfect agitator.

Everything crystallizes in my mind the way it normally does when I chance upon a discovery that changes the course of my research. The volcanic land. The mines. The mercury in my blood. The changing of an entire society. None of these should happen. Fractured items come together to form a whole.

This isn't a mass extinction event but a dedicated, intentional, slow mass murder. So slow that nobody has noticed. And who would after six centuries? But why would it be a slow murder? The Ulgix are technologically advanced. They have the means to exterminate the population in days—why not do just that? Maybe they had with the systematic extermination of the stronger subspecies on the planet, leaving only the weak and easily trodden.

I grip Rif's large hand in mine and look into his confused, serious eyes to deliver news he probably doesn't want to hear. "The Ulgix are killing you and this is how they're doing it. This is the origin of The Death."

Chapter Thirteen

Rhifgraugdk

My body goes as numb as my mind as I stare around the cavern hidden away beneath my stronghold. I almost can't believe such a thing is here and for a moment, I worry for my sanity. However, both Stef and Jet stare at everything with a combination of the same awe and horror rearing through me.

Why would this be here? How is this even here? D'Kali has never given me any indication of what is taking place beneath our very feet.

My omega takes my hand and her words deliver the killing blow. *The Ulgix are killing you and this is how they're doing it.* I share a look with my bond brothers. More questions crowd my mind as my omega fills me in.

"I'd have to test it, but it's more than probably mercury. The color is very distinctive. It occurs naturally in the earth's crust. It's released through volcanic activity and the weathering of rocks. Your land is all volcanic activity, which is how they've mined mercury so easily," she says.

I don't follow everything that she says, but I let her speak. Her eyes glow and she's animated in a way I haven't seen before. It's better than the lost, soul-deep sadness that has enveloped her, and my heart sinks because I know we're responsible for the latter. It's taken a travesty and a life-threatening situation for me to understand what I've done.

She blinks up at me and I'm so lost in her exotic blue eyes I almost don't hear what she says. "It happened in Japan between 1932 and 1968. A factory producing acetic acid high in methylmercury discharged the waste into Minamata Bay. The shellfish and fish ate the mercury and people ate the fish. Disease spread in their community and they couldn't work out why. At least fifty thousand people were affected, and more than two thousand cases of disease were certified. It peaked in the 1950s with severe cases of brain damage, paralysis, and delirium. It may not affect your species in quite the same way given our biological differences, but it is affecting you. The infertility. Systematic dying out and reduction of your population. It all adds up."

I don't follow the dates or the places she's described. "What adds up?" I'm about to call her omega, but I stop myself in time. I want to see her eyes light up, not dull so she wastes away.

Her face shutters for a moment and then softens. "You're being poisoned, Rif. The Ulgix are putting the mercury you mine into your water supply. You drink it. You bathe in it. It's making your people sick and infertile. The changes in your society aren't natural. You're being systematically and slowly killed." She stabs her finger at the vast waterfalls. "And this is how they're doing it. You have to stop this or more of your people will die."

"How do you know?" Jet asks.

"I'm a biomedical scientist. It's my job to come up with cures for diseases, and to do that I have to understand poisons such as mercury as well as a host of other factors. I . . . help find cures for diseases that kill thousands of my people. That's my job," she says.

There's something poignant and sad about her. A deep wound that has never healed. The same wound in me recognizes it, but only because it's similar.

Only because I've been forced to look inside myself and recognize it.

There's so much I've missed about this female. Her job is to save lives. I wonder how many people suffer because she's here. She isn't a normal omega. She's so much more.

My gaze slides to my bond brothers. Jet wears his emotions openly, and I can clearly see he's just as affected by her words as I am. Stef moves toward her, wanting to hold her and comfort her. He barely holds himself back.

She sighs. "That's how I know what mercury is and that ingesting it will kill. Mercury is in my blood work and if it isn't stopped, it will kill me. It will kill us all."

The numbness in my mind drains away to be replaced with rage as hot as the underground lava belts in my land. I try to find the logic and reason behind why they would do this to us, but the ugly truth is obvious. I'm an alpha warlord and I rule Rjúkaland. I should know what the Ulgix are doing, but I don't. I should know this facility is here, but I don't. What else don't I know? How much has D'Kali kept from me? What is he really doing to us?

"D'Kali has lied to us," I whisper.

D'Kali, whom I've known all my life. My trusted advisor who comforted me when my parents died. Who comforted my parents and their parents when the same happened to them. He's been a constant in my family line for generations. I don't think twice about trusting him. Why would I when my great-great-great grandparents trusted him? He's a tie to my past, so long-lived he's shared stories of my ancestors whom I'd never have known otherwise.

A part of me doesn't want to acknowledge what is clearly in front of my eyes. I don't want to admit I've been so blind. That in helping D'Kali, I've been killing my own people.

"Why would they do this?" Stef says. He sounds as adrift as I am. He's lost family members. None of our brethren are unaffected. "If they needed something from us, why didn't they just ask for our help instead of killing us all off?"

"Because they knew whatever they wanted can't be handed over. It must be taken. It can only be taken by stealth and subterfuge," Jet says.

D'Kali's betrayal is a sword that cuts me to the bone. I can't pull my eyes from the Ulgix poisoning our water. This is right below the stronghold. Every drop goes to our people. Our livestock. Our fields. This is treachery at its most base. This isn't opportunistic. This is well-thought-out. D'Kali has seen thousands of lives lost and has kept his secret close to his chest.

The deepest part of his deception is that he's willingly made our omega sick. It's no wonder she's stuck in pre-heat. D'Kali is causing her harm, and for that, he won't live to see another day.

"I will destroy this. I'll destroy every Ulgix who steps foot in here. They will all die to pay for their crimes against our people." I force the words between clenched teeth.

"Those are the sweetest words I've heard you say, brother," Jet says.

"D'Kali," Stef snarls and points.

My vision streams with red as I watch the tall figure of D'Kali slip into a room beyond the waterfalls. My muscles swell with rage, and venom drips from my fangs when I see the betas from the mine through a window into the lab. They're strapped to sleek metal cots and have tubes running from their bodies to the overhead medical machines I'm familiar with from his lab. As D'Kali enters the room, a scream tears through the open door.

I watch the scene unfold. One of the betas convulses. Red foam sprays from his mouth. His horns lengthen and his body swells in a way that's unnatural for a beta. His muscles become more defined. His feet dangle off the end of the cot, where moments before they were nowhere near the end.

"He's turning the beta into an alpha," Stef rasps.

D'Kali injects the beta, who tips back his head and opens his mouth in a scream we can't hear. Blood seeps from where his skin splits. The male contorts and I see white bone emerging from his joints. The beta sags, as if defeated, and blood drips to the floor.

A holographic display appears above the body. D'Kali makes some adjustments to the illustration and moves to the next beta, who struggles against his restraints and watches with wide, rounded eyes. His mouth moves and I know he's pleading with D'Kali for mercy.

My omega sucks in a sharp breath. She clutches her shirt and looks up at me with wild eyes. I can see all the white around the blue. "God. He changed that guy's DNA only to kill him."

I understand enough of what she said to make me sick to my stomach. D'Kali isn't stopping. He'll kill every beta in the room. There's no telling how much blood is on his hands after six centuries.

A shout sounds from across the cavern. We've been discovered. At least twenty Ulgix charge toward us. There are only the three of us to protect our omega.

We'll be enough. We have to be.

Rage bleeds through me, and my muscles swell to aid my fight. The bloodlust streaking through me from the battle with my feral alphas rises from where it was simmering just below the surface. I withdraw my swords from the sheaths on my back and bare my fangs. I'll rip through the traitors with my swords, claws, and fangs.

A hand tugs the long blade at my hip. "Give me that," my omega demands. I'm helpless but to do as she requests, even though I don't want her to hurt herself with it.

I draw the blade free and give her the handle. "This is sharp, omega."

My lips thin and I'm reminded of my slipup. She hates the term omega. But then she grips the sword with both hands and swings it through the air. "Don't worry. Fifteen years of kendo."

I don't know what this "kendo" is, but surprise merges with a bolt of lust and shoots through me. I force it down because I don't want to fight with a hard cock, but I will revisit this. "Later, you'll tell me how you know how to use my blade."

She grins, baring her non-lethal, even white teeth. My cock swells again, determined to take over my body. "*Your* blade?"

I'm happy to give her my blade. I'll give her anything. I'll have my blacksmith make a sword specially weighted for her if she'll smile at me like that again.

"Stay behind us at all times," Stef barks before stepping in front of our omega. I take his side and Jet falls in beside me. This is our usual formation. We've spent most of our lives fighting like this, but this is the only fight where we've ever had anything as precious as our omega to keep safe. Without her, we're nothing.

I push aside my worry that we won't be strong enough. We have to be and it won't help what I have to do. There is no other outcome I'll accept. The first Ulgix reach us. I step forward, raise my sword into the air, and slash through the male's chest. Blood sprays and he collapses in a limp pile of broken limbs. My rage simmers and adds fuel to my bloodlust.

A flash of blue light streaks toward us. Jet pulls our omega to the ground and covers her with his body as the wall behind me explodes. Shards of granite shatter around us, cutting my clothing and skin.

Blood drips down the side of Stef's face as he stands in front of Jet and the omega. Another Ulgix lifts a sleek weapon and aims at us.

"Rif, get down!" our omega screams as the Ulgix pulls the trigger and another blue light streaks toward me.

Chapter Fourteen

Adele

Rif moves inhumanly fast. He should—he's an alien and not human at all—but their bodies have swelled to at least another third of their already huge body mass. Their muscles bulge and strain beneath taut, smooth skin. They are natural killing machines, predators, and I realize just how gentle they've been with me compared to what they are now.

The cords on Jet's neck strain, and sweat shines on his skin. He picks me up and runs as Rif slides out of the way, and the laser streaks past him. Another crater opens in the wall where his head had been. Stef's roar merges with Rif's as they charge into the fray.

Jet places me behind a machine. "Stay here." I intend to. I'm good with a sword, but the alphas are something else altogether. A real fight is nothing like the staged fight in a dojo. I know my way around a katana, but I've never used a weapon to hurt another person.

I nod and he runs to join Rif and Stef. My eyes can barely track their movements. Their swords are natural extensions of their limbs. They're dancing with a lethal abandon, each movement flowing into the next with deadly precision. They twist, duck, weave, and spin. No movement is wasted. Nothing is a mistake. They judge with accurate precision and all three move as a singular unit. Protect, spin, dart, slash.

Even armed with laser weapons I've only seen in science-fiction movies, the Ulgix don't stand a chance against the ferocity of my alphas. The floor is now a lake of blood, severed limbs, and still bodies. The creature in me watches from behind my eyes. Her approval simmers and lust makes my pussy throb with inappropriate desire. These are worthy alphas. I know I shouldn't feel this way. It's not logical, but I can't take my eyes off them. This is absolute carnage and I'm entranced.

The heat which I've forgotten about flares up. Sweat trickles into my eyes as perspiration breaks out across my body. My abdomen twists and I tense through a cramp that steals my breath.

My alphas dash toward me. I see through blurry eyes that all the Ulgix who had launched the attack are now dead. I rise to my feet, trying to hide the violent spasms. Rif grabs my hand and holds me steady. "Omega?"

I don't care that he's called me that name. The creature in me preens. I don't have the energy to ignore her, but a part of me doesn't care to. The instant he touches me, the cramp rolls into a wave of lust. Wetness seeps from my core and dampens the tops of my thighs.

"I'm okay," I say, and hope he blames my breathless tone on the true terror of our situation and not my incongruous hunger.

Stef's nostrils flare and I know he's scenting the sweetness and accompanying slick sliding out of me. I know I should care, but the truth is, I don't. I like the hunger in their eyes and the way they're looking at me as though I'm the center of their universe. They fought for me and it's my right to claim them. I don't question that, either. It's merely a fact.

"Omega." Jet's voice is gravel. His thick tone is longing, craving, and dark promise all rolled into one. I sway toward him, unable to stop myself.

Rif curses. "We need to stop D'Kali."

I catch myself before I plaster my body against Jet. And then Stef. And Rif. I flatten my palm against the machine I hid behind, grounding myself with its coolness. We can't let D'Kali get away. The betas suffered at his hand, and the creature in me won't stand for that.

My wrath becomes hers as she lets me straighten. The cramping subsides, although not all the way, as it has done before. It hints at what is to come, but I can't think about that yet. "He needs to die for what he's done," I say.

That's not me. I don't want those things. My life has been about saving lives, but the part of me taking over is different. This kill is justified.

"As you wish," Stef says.

"He's still in the lab with the betas," Jet says as he peeks around the equipment we're hiding behind.

I'm surprised he didn't hear the bloodbath, but the lab is presumably soundproofed.

"Follow me. Keep our female between us at all times, and don't let her out of your sight," Rif says.

I follow him as he skirts the wall and moves toward the lab. Their eyes track everywhere, watching for threats and ready to take action. Tension thrums through all of us, and I grip the sword Rif gave me in my sweating palm.

We crouch under the window and edge along to the door. Rif gestures and slaps his palm on the screen on the wall. When the door slides open, he leaps through the threshold and cuts the head off the closest Ulgix.

Stef's arms band about my waist and he carries me through the door as Jet takes position in front of me. My vision is filled with his back as Rif and Stef cut through the Ulgix lab assistants.

D'Kali races to the bank of screens, and an alarm blares through both the lab and the cavern. A new swarm of Ulgix charges through the open door. Jet springs into action to stop them from reaching me. Many Ulgix converge on Rif and Stef. My alphas are extreme predators, but the odds are stacked so unevenly. Blood sprays the lab, coating the floor and the walls, and not all of it belongs to the Ulgix.

"Omega!" The beta on the closest table calls to me. "Release our restraints. Please."

Sweat beads his brow, and he's trembling. His gaze bounces to my fighting alphas and back to me. He's desperate and might be our only chance. He's no longer quite a beta. Up close I can see the differences. He's halfway between the bulk of an alpha, and not quite as small and wiry as he'd once been either.

Using Rif's sword, I slice through the metal. The cuffs peel back from the beta's wrists as I make short work of his ankles. "Free the others. They'll help."

He pushes off the side of the cot and launches himself into an Ulgix. He swings a fist and smashes it into the face of another Ulgix. Whatever D'Kali did to the beta is now working against the reptile.

I dart to the next cot and release the other betas. They disappear into the battle and fight alongside my alphas. They roar in anger as they unleash their aggression, which I can't blame them for. D'Kali has put them through hell.

Talking about D'Kali . . . I press my back against the wall and try to keep out of the way of fists and laser bolts. The lab is filled to the brim with Ulgix and Amadonians. The scent of blood and burned rubber fills my nose, and my stomach boils.

I edge along and find D'Kali at the same controls he set the alarm off with. He's doing something to the screens. Rif's roar vibrates through me as he throws the body of an Ulgix toward D'Kali. The body slams into the screens. He falls to the ground, but the screen cracks, the lights flicker and die. The system is completely destroyed.

D'Kali's face contorts into a sneer. His yellow eyes narrow and his lips draw back to show long, pointed teeth. His tongue darts out before drawing back into his mouth. Before my eyes, he changes from a simpering sycophant to something dangerous. He pulls out a laser gun and points it directly at Rif, who's engaged in a battle with two Ulgix.

I'm on the other side of the room. The battle is between the both of us, and Rif is unaware he's in D'Kali's sights. I'm useless here. I can't even throw my sword at him. If only I had a laser gun.

At my feet is a severed arm and at the end of the arm is a laser gun held in the tight grip of a hand without an owner. I drop to my knees and wrench the gun free. I stagger back to my feet and fire.

The blue laser hits D'Kali in his shoulder. He crashes into the wall behind him, blood blooming on his white lab coat. His arm flies to the side and the gun drops from his grip. He pins me with narrowed eyes. I aim the gun at him again, this time at his head, but too late as a body slams into me.

I'm taken to the ground. An Ulgix in a white coat lands on top of me. The back of my head slams into the ground. Black dots cross my vision. A heavy weight crushes my chest, but almost before I'm aware of it, a roar shakes the foundation of the room. The weight disappears and I draw a breath to see Stef snatching up the Ulgix. Blood sprays over me as he tears the arms off the body and tosses them aside. He spares it no more attention before he's on his knees next to me.

"Omega!" His hands pat my body and it takes me a couple of tries to catch my breath.

"I'm okay," I wheeze.

Bodies are thrown behind Stef. Blood splatters in wide arcs, hitting the floor, the walls, everyone. The flashes of laser bolts vanish and silence fills the room. Stef picks me up and holds me close, a tremor running through his body.

Bodies line the floor, but they're all Ulgix. The betas stagger over the bodies, kicking them for signs of life. Rif pins D'Kali to the wall by his throat. Jet takes me from Stef and crushes me to his chest.

"I'm okay. I'm all right," I say.

He buries his nose in the juncture of my neck and shoulder and breathes me in. His fingers splay over my back as he stands and simply holds me against him. A wave of heat corkscrews through me, but the pain is distant. My muscles contract and relax in rhythmic waves, leaving a needy wake when they relax. I reach for Stef and tug him toward me, satisfied when I'm jammed between them. It's not quite good enough without Rif, but this does enough for now.

Stef claps his hand on Jet's shoulder. "She's unharmed, brother, but the battle isn't over just yet. Rif has D'Kali. We're due some answers before our brother rips him apart."

Jet takes his fill of my scent, tucks me more securely against his side, and turns to Rif. I don't care about his blood-soaked clothes. I clutch him. He's injured, but alive.

"Why have you betrayed us?" Rif's voice is hoarse. His pain pulls a thread in my chest and makes it my own. A keening wail unwinds. This being is responsible for the fall of a complex society, resulting in millions of deaths. He's a despicable creature who deserves to rot in the darkest, coldest reaches of the afterlife.

D'Kali chuffs and I realize he's laughing. A churning wave of rage peaks inside of me. How dare he laugh in the face of such tragedy. How dare he do anything but beg for our forgiveness. "You may have discovered this, but it's too late to stop. You're too late to do anything but suffer the consequences of your apathy."

"We trusted you . . . *I* trusted you," Rif says.

"The great alpha warlord. The pinnacle of your barbarian race. You should be thankful you're only a cog in the machine for something far greater than yourself." D'Kali coughs. Blood splatters over his lips and runs in a string of saliva from the corner of his mouth. Looks like I did more damage to him than his shoulder. In fact, I don't know how he's still alive. I didn't quite shoot his shoulder. The middle of his chest is soaked with his blood, quickly spreading down his body. His green scales turn pale yellow with every passing second.

Trickles of blood run down D'Kali's neck where Rif's claws puncture his skin and join the mess that is his chest. Rif's hand trembles as he struggles to hold himself back from ripping D'Kali's head from his shoulders. "I may be a barbarian, but I will be the barbarian who ends your miserable life."

"I've lived . . . off the lifeblood . . . of your forefathers. Never stop . . . us." D'Kali chokes and goes limp.

Rif roars. His hand grasps the top of D'Kali's head and twists. A snap echoes around the room, and D'Kali's head tilts to an unnatural angle. He throws the reptile's body to the ground, his great chest heaving. A vast hole opens inside me and his anguish becomes mine.

Jet's hand folds around my neck and he presses his forehead against mine. Another thread burrows its way into the darkness, brought to me through shared sorrow. He holds me still, fighting to contain his composure when I know a storm rages inside him.

Stef presses against my side and I slide my fingers into his hair as his arms band about my middle. His heart pounds against my shoulder and I tighten my grip, tangling the strands around my hand. His despair is drawn into me, sucked there with our misery.

Whatever all three feel echoes inside me. The creature rises on a wave of their pain, too fast and strong for me to hold back. I loosen the reins that I've clutched so tightly all this time. They slip from my mental grip as though they never existed. As though the creature was only humoring me and allowed me to think I controlled her, when the opposite was true all along.

She fills the empty space, and more, I never knew existed. The cells in my body are incinerated and replaced with something more. Something other. I'm myself, but I'm not. I've emerged from the newborn state of my arrival here. The strange needs and desires that dogged me are now mine. I take them on with relish because this is what I am, and because what I am crystallizes into perfect sense. The two halves I've battled since I woke up in that field are cohesive.

I am female. I am *omega*.

My sense of self is sharp and focused. I've shed my cocoon and emerged changed.

I cry out when my stomach cramps once again. The emptiness in my chest moves deep into my abdomen. A river of slick pours from me and my core throbs. Empty. So empty. I writhe in Jet's arms, trying to grind my pussy against his hard muscles. I need to be filled. I need my alphas' cocks. I need their seed. I need to be bred.

I pull Stef's hair. I scratch Jet's shoulder and cry out for Rif. One word rises from me, a plaintive order I know they will obey. "Please."

Rif dashes toward me, his face awash with awe, hunger, and fierce male satisfaction. The carnage around us is forgotten under his full focus. "Omega." His deep voice makes me shiver. Slick gushes from me and coats Jet's stomach, and I don't care. Sweet apple blossom perfumes around us, signifying my need and demanding my alphas' attention.

Rif doesn't hesitate. He tugs his fingers through my hair. I gasp with the sting when the pain becomes easy pleasure. He takes my mouth in his. His tongue sweeps into my mouth in a commanding kiss that I have no desire to end. Stef and Jet close around me, and I'm enfolded in cedar, sandalwood, and leather. The sharp pain drains away to be replaced by a deep, driving ache. I writhe against them, delirious with arousal.

Rif pulls back but I chase him because I wasn't finished with the kiss. He holds me back with his tight grip in my hair. "You'll get more kisses. You'll get our mouths, our fangs, our hands, and our cocks. You'll get all of us. Finally, omega, you're in heat."

Chapter Fifteen

Adele

Heat.

The word hooks into the deepest part of me. Anticipation arches through me, and my world rights to spin under a new axis. I'm not afraid anymore; instead, I'm greedy for it. I can hold nothing back. I don't want to.

Want.

The word is pale compared to the blinding desire arching through me. My brain can't string words together, but I find one that describes it all. I grind my pussy against Jet's muscles. Spirals fill my belly, but I still pulse with emptiness.

"Need." My voice is a plaintive plea. I fist Stef's electric-blue plaits and tug. His eyes narrow and burn. A thrill races through me at the hard gleam he spears me with.

Rif grips the back of my head and tips it back. "Bad omega. You'll get what you need without hurting your alphas."

I bare my teeth and thrust my breasts out, my nipples diamond points. They throb with a needy, sharp pain. I arch up to bite him, but he holds me steady with a strict tug that makes my pussy clench.

Breed.

I don't know what they're waiting for. They know I need them. My clothes are too tight. Too constricting. I have to close my eyes against the too-bright light. I tear at the neck of the shirt I'm wearing. It's strangling me. I don't want to wear this itchy clothing. I want their silky skin and their hot tongues, their bodies slippery with our combined sweat. I want to be filled to the brim with their cum. That's exactly what I need to warm the cold emptiness where my womb exists.

Submit.

I stop trying to hiss and bite, and let my body relax. Six strong arms hold me up. The tip of Jet's hard cock prods my backside. Stef grinds himself against my hip, and Rif tips my head to the side and licks a path along my neck. I shiver as the wake of heat cools.

"Good omega," he growls in my ear.

The logical part of my mind should be incensed at those words. Instead, I gush slick and coat Jet's abdomen because the greater part of me wants to be his good girl. I should be embarrassed, but I can't find it in myself to feel anything other than raging arousal. I grind down, needing to find the elusive release I'm seeking. I can't get enough friction however hard I press against him. A thin, needy sound breaks from me. I'm so empty. I'll go insane if I'm not filled. I scratch Jet's back, getting more desperate with each passing moment.

"We have to get her back to my rooms before she sinks too far into her heat," Rif barks.

Jet presses my nose into his neck and squeezes me against him. I suck his scent into my lungs and cling to him. He strides past bodies, but none of the horror affects me. I don't care about them. All I care about are my alphas and their touch, their attention, and tempering the infernal heat coursing through me.

Humid air coats me as we walk into the open. It's a relief and yet not, because it's not exactly where I want to be. My pussy flutters and my abdomen cramps so hard and fast I almost choke. This cramp is different from the others. It's a hot blade that sinks through me. The other cramps, as bad as they were, were nothing like this. If they don't stop, the pain might kill me. If I'm not filled soon, I might cut out my own womb.

I struggle against Jet's arms, needing . . . wanting . . . something . . . The urge is indefinable. It overrules everything. *Want. Need. Alphas.* Yes, that's exactly what I need, so why aren't they giving me what I demand?

I hiss and clamp my teeth into Jet's shoulder, showing him how much pain I'm in. I'll make him hurt as much as I'm hurting. It makes no sense and yet makes perfect sense.

Jet crushes me against him, his fingers holding my head and neck still. Another hand strokes up and down my back, soothing me. Jet sets me on my feet, and I find we're back in Rif's rooms. They step away from me, watching, waiting. For what, I don't know. They should be *tending* to me. I take a step toward Stef, stop, and twist around.

I spy the bed in the middle of the vast room. My nostrils flare. Our combined scents on the bed help soothe the claws that want to break free, but only just. There's something wrong with it. A snarl rises from my lips and I throw all the bedding from the mattress. I don't even see it all land on the floor. I'm too busy smoothing the remaining sheet. I drag my nose along the material, hovering above a patch where my slick has soaked. I detect the strains of cedar, sandalwood, and leather. Acceptable.

Home.

I tuck the sheet along the corners of the bed until every crease is gone. Something is missing, but I don't know what it is.

"Omega."

I snarl and turn toward the voice. I'm ready to launch myself across the room until I see the material Stef holds. I inhale, taking in my alphas' scents and the scent-free material he's holding.

I move from the bed and rip it from his hand. I hold it to my face. The strands are so soft against my cheek. Perfect. I take the fur to the bed and arrange it just so. It's not enough. There is a jumbled pile of materials in the room's corner.

I stalk to the pile and rip through it. I take acceptable materials and throw away some that are too scratchy, too light, or too heavy. I take them to the bed and tuck and roll them into an edge that fits just right. I don't know how long this takes me, but I only stop when it feels right.

I've woven an oval wall around the edge of the mattress and piled it with the softest pillows. I don't know how I've created something like this, but I have, and that's all that matters.

The heat simmering in the background rises to full force once more. I rip the clothing from my body and throw it to the floor. *Need. Want. Alpha.*

I swing around to see my alphas pacing along the wall of the room. Their lips pull back and reveal glinting fangs. They are already naked, something that soothes the beast inside me. Their bodies have swelled, revealing their bulging muscles and taut crimson skin. Their cocks are fully erect. Long. Thick. They leak pre-cum. Their balls swing heavily beneath their thick thighs.

My mouth waters as my womb clamps. I want them, so why aren't they coming to soothe the increasingly painful ache inside me? I hiss my displeasure.

Rif's black eyes burn. His thighs ping as he forces himself to stand on the spot. "You have to invite us into your nest, omega. Then we can give you everything you want. We'll fill you with our cocks, claim you and breed you, but we can't do that without your invitation."

The last part of my logical mind finds a way to shoot through the fog. "No claim."

The muscle ticks at his jaw as he grinds his teeth. Light flashes in the backs of his eyes as Stef and Jet stop in their tracks. They stare at me and I almost choke on the tension rising in waves, but the part of me that has chosen to rise stands firm. She—*I*—can't lose myself to that.

Rif nods his head, but his eyes never leave mine. A drop of pre-cum falls to the floor, making my mouth water. Waste. That drop needed to be in my mouth. My cunt. I will take everything they can give. "If that's what you wish, omega. We'll take you in every way you'll let us, but we won't claim you. Now get into your nest and invite us in."

His voice has dropped to a dangerous growl. Slick runs down my thighs. The creature consumes the logical part of me until I'm nothing more than instinct and need.

I climb into my nest as the alphas move to surround me, part my thighs, and bare myself to their eyes. Their gazes drop to the most intimate part of my body and I preen, a puddle of slick oozing from me to pool under my backside. My thighs glisten with my arousal, and the sweet apple-blossom scent perfumes the room. I hold out my arms to them and say the only thing that's important. "Please, alphas."

Chapter Sixteen

Stefnan

Our omega is in full heat. Only a rim of light-blue remains around the dark center of her eyes. My muscles twitch as I work to contain myself. My painfully hard cock pulses with each beat of my heart, but I won't fail my omega. I'll wait until she asks us into her nest.

I never thought I would be in this position. Never entertained the idea that I would ever have an omega of my own. This small female from another planet is my savior.

"Please, alphas." Her plea spears and hooks into my heart. I climb over the wall of her carefully constructed nest with my bond brothers, taking care not to disrupt her hard work. And what a work of art it is.

My cock leaked constantly as I watched her create this masterpiece. I had to remove my too-constricting clothes. I close my fingers around my cock and strangle it to keep my feet where they are and not rush to the omega that everything inside me calls for. I remembered my fathers telling me never to interrupt an omega when she's building her nest. It's a personal construction in which she will invite only the alphas she deems worthy.

There were moments when I hesitated, caught in my head. Fear assaulted me, thinking she might not ask me. What if she found me unworthy? What if I had to watch as she issued an invitation to my bond brothers and not me? What if I had failed her in some way?

The list was endless. I was barely able to keep recent events from overwhelming me, but I needed to. Our omega was the most important being in our lives.

On our way to Rif's rooms, he rounded up Lodin and the rest of our alpha warriors to make sure the secret cavern beneath our very feet is taken care of. If our omega hadn't gone into heat, we would be leading them down there. I'm sure I'll move past the rage that consumes me, but that won't be until after our omega's heat when I'll track down any unfound Ulgix and shred their bodies with my claws for the threat to my omega alone.

I lie next to our omega while Jet lies on her other side. She opens her arms and welcomes us to her body. Jet clasps her jaw while I descend on her pink pebbled nipple. I suck it into my mouth and lave the bead with my tongue. Her scent intensifies on her skin, filling my mouth with her sweetness. I'm careful with my fangs so as not to scratch her. Venom drips onto her skin, but I lick it up. She's asked us not to claim her, and while I'll abide by her wishes, I have to shove aside the driving need and hurt that she asked us not to do what is natural. Not to claim her.

Our omega isn't used to being an omega. D'Kali has more to answer for. If Rif hadn't twisted his skull half off his head, I would have tortured him for more answers first. No matter. There will be Ulgix yet to round up, I'm sure. Plenty of bodies to take my anger out on and for questions to be answered. The cavern was too large and too well-organized for the handful of Ulgix we killed to be all there was.

For now, I devour my omega's breast and knead the other peak. I won't tarnish my omega's heat with thoughts of deception. I'll do my best to make her change her mind about claiming her. I'll demand her full surrender—her mind and her body. Nothing else will be acceptable.

I take her other breast in my hand, massaging her tender flesh to bring her pleasure, while Jet lashes her mouth with his tongue.

"How good you look being tended by your alphas," Rif says. He steps over the lip of her nest and kneels between her legs. Slick glistens on her thighs, and her hips rise and squirm as she becomes more desperate. Her belly undulates and she's almost in the grip of another blinding cramp.

My mouth pops away from her breast. "Don't tease, Rif. Give her what she needs."

He glances at me and quickly back to between her thighs, reaching out and sliding a finger along her slit. A moan drags up her throat, to be kissed away by Jet. Her legs twitch and her hips rise from the bedding.

If Rif takes any longer, I'll shove him out of the way and do what she's begging for us to do, but Rif is a good alpha. His eyes roll to the back of his head as he sucks his finger dry. I'm almost jealous because I want her flavor to coat my tongue, but he flattens himself on his belly, splays her legs with his wide shoulders, and works to devour her.

My beautiful, responsive omega tenses and screams her release. My cock jerks. I fist it and smear pre-cum over her hip. I slide a drop off the tip with my thumb and jam it between both her and Jet's mouths.

Her tongue curls around my digit and she sucks. The thrill goes through me and tugs deep within my balls. I have to hold on to my cum because my omega will demand to be filled. I do, only by the grace of the gods and my will to please her.

I need to taste her now. I suck her breast and trail my fingers down her heaving body to where Rif is feasting. I glide my fingers through the slippery mess between her thighs, paying attention to the little pink nubbin, swirling around it and grinding down when another moan is pulled from her.

Her little hands tighten in my hair, bringing a sting to my scalp. The small pain is both relief and pleasure. I move to feast on her other breast, holding it still in my palm. I let my claws dimple her skin and listen to her pounding heart. I milk my cock with my other hand and can't help pumping my hips against her thigh.

Her small hand skates from where she's clutching my hair and moves between our bodies. She's doing the same to Jet and I realize what she's trying to find. I move my cock into her hand. Her small fingers squeeze my erect shaft. Bliss fills me. I put my hand around hers and help her to twist and stroke.

She turns her head and looks into my eyes as her hand fucks my erection. "You're the most beautiful omega to ever have existed." I sound like Jet, but I don't care because it's true.

I cup her cheek and kiss her, sliding my tongue into her willing mouth. I'm lost to this omega and I can only count it as a blessing. She has my heart in her tiny hand. She doesn't need to ask for anything from me. It's freely given before she will ever feel the need.

Jaetvard

My omega's hand feels like the heavens on my cock. Her dainty fingers can barely fit around my girth, but I'll accept anything she can give me. I watch as Rif's head ducks between her thighs. My lucky brother is able to drink from the source, but I don't mind because it's what she needs, and I will get my turn. My fathers said an omega's heat can last for days, so I'm happy for Rif to take the first drink, knowing there will be plenty for all of us.

Her hand works Stef's cock. He's as large in her hand as I am. She breaks their kiss as Stef throws back his head and clenches his face. I know he's close to coming and trying to hold back as much as he can so he can gift our omega with his cum in her cunt.

I rise onto my knees and throw one leg over her shoulders. Her eyes flare and her mouth opens in a perfect O at my unexpected move, before those blown orbs drop to my cock.

"Take me in your mouth. Suck me," I say. My voice is nothing more than a hoarse whisper.

I aim the tip at her mouth and feed her as much as I dare as she leans forward and swallows me with a greedy whine. I don't want to hurt her with my girth, so I hold on to my knot and dip the tip into her mouth.

Her pink tongue darts out to lick me and when I put more of myself into her mouth, the suction makes my whole body shiver.

She moves away from the end of my length, which is glistening with her saliva, and looks up at me with an expression that makes my heart melt. "I want your cum in my mouth, alpha. Please, give me your cum."

"I can't deny you, omega. What you want, you shall have," I say.

She hums around my cock when I line myself up with her mouth. Stef licks and plays with her breasts under my thighs and I feel every electric jolt that Rif sends through her body. I hope she doesn't clamp down on me with those even white teeth, but then she sucks and all care slips from me.

Her mouth is divine. "So good, omega. You suck me so good."

She groans and the vibrations travel up my cock and into my balls. They draw up tight. My cock pulses as pleasure slams up my backbone from where she's latched around me. Hot cum spills from me. She drinks until I can't pump any more into her. She swallows as much as she can, but my cum seeps from her mouth and dribbles down her chin. I feel waves of her own pleasure break through her as her back bows. Stef groans and wet heat splashes onto her waist.

"Good, omega. See how well you're taking him," Stef praises her.

I withdraw from her mouth and ease off her body. I kiss her and taste my essence mixed with her flavor on her mouth. She sighs and her eyes fall shut.

Stef massages his cum into her skin until it disappears. She needs as much from us as she can get. Rif rises from between her thighs, his jaw glistening with her release. His long crimson tongue laps her juices from his chin. His face is a mix of sated pleasure and intense focus. I think his expression matches the one I wear, too.

Our omega's eyes flick open and lock on Rif's erection. In a move I don't expect, she comes to her knees, plants her hands on his thighs, and takes his cock into her mouth.

Rhifgraugdk

A groan rips from me when our omega pounces on me. Her wet mouth descends on my cock. I hope she doesn't hurt herself, so I hold my cock steady for her to feast on. Her mouth burns as hot as her sweating skin. She hums as her head bobs up and down, but soon her hips undulate and I know exactly what she needs.

"Take her cunt, Stef. Then you, Jet. She'll need all of us," I rasp. Her sweet mouth on me is bliss. She'll need us to care for her every need while she's in heat. I almost can't believe I have this time with her and my bond brothers, as D'Kali nearly took her away from us.

I burn to think of the Ulgix's deception, and I make a silent vow to make them pay, but I'm hovering on the cusp of rut. Lodin and his team will be able to take care of any remaining Ulgix and any of the lesser alphas who succumbed to our omega's scent. I'll get to the bottom of their actions and make them pay for their travesty.

Stef moves behind our omega. His cock is fully erect and ready to tend to her. He's so large over her bent form. We're all so big compared to her, and I wonder how I'll be able to stuff my shaft into her, but omega bodies are made to take alpha cocks.

The moment he runs his cock through her slippery folds and hovers at her entrance, she releases my member, shudders, and turns around. She presses back against him, trying to impale herself in her desperation.

"Please, please, please." Her words are a whispered plea.

I take her chin and make her look up at me. Her lips are pink and puffy, and her eyes liquid globes of need. "I want you to look at me when Stef fully gives you his cock. I want to see the moment he enters your channel and gives you what you need."

Her gaze holds steady with mine. Her eyes flutter, but she manages to keep them open as Stef works himself into her tight little body.

Stef groans when his quads are flush to the back of her delicate thighs. His fingers wrap around her tiny waist, folding around her in a vise-like grip. "Gods . . . feels . . . so good."

Our omega whimpers and tries to move, but she can't get far between both of us. "Stef will give your cunt his cock and I'll give your mouth my cock. You'll bear it until I give you permission to cum. Do you hear me?"

She gives me a quick nod and sucks down my offering. Stef slides out at the same time as I do and together we slam back into her. Her moan is drawn from deep within her stomach, and I feel the shockwave of Stef's hips jolting her. I withdraw from her mouth. She takes a quick breath before I push myself deep into her mouth and down her throat. She swallows around me. The convulsing muscles are pure bliss. I can't get enough of her. I'll never get enough, and that is okay with me. I don't want to. I want to be there on my dying day, giving her the pleasure she demands.

I trail my fingers along her smooth, pale skin. So different from my leathery hide. She's gorgeous. Sensuous. And she's all ours.

Stef's thrusts grow more erratic. She writhes between us. She clamps her hands around my knot and tries to force it into her mouth. It'll be too big and she'll suffocate. I wrap my thumb and forefinger around my cock to stop her from swallowing me. Each of Stef's thrusts bumps her mouth into my hand.

I sense Stef is near completion and allow bliss to wash over me too. My thighs tremble as liquid sensation rolls through me. My balls feel like they're exploding as cum rushes down my shaft. She sucks and swallows everything I can give her. Every last drop goes down her throat, where I know it will nourish her heat.

She releases my cock, panting. Her face is scrunched up and she throws back her head as Stef grinds himself into her cunt. Her mouth opens and she keens, the sound strangling my shaft, as Stef's knot inflates inside her body.

He grips her hips, his claws dimpling her skin, throws back his head, and roars loud enough to alert the stronghold to the taking of our omega. It's justified. Let them all know. This will give them hope. His body bows and his long, brilliant locs dangle down his back.

His chest inflates like a bellows as he finally stops coming. Our omega goes limp. I help him gather her form against him and position her alongside his body, taking care not to jostle where they're joined. I stretch out her legs and Stef entwines them, and his arm bands around her waist. She's deeply asleep as Stef gives me a weary, satisfied smile before he drops off too. I slide between Jet and our omega and let sleep claim me.

Adele

I wake and begin to writhe. The pleasant, satisfying pressure in my core isn't there anymore, and I'm filled with need. I inhale the scent of my alphas. It helps to soothe me, but I need much more than scent.

Rif's black eyes fill my vision. Sleepy one moment and fully alert the next. My abdomen twists and my achy nipples bead under his full focus. Full arousal slams into me. I move my thighs from where my legs are tangled and wrap them around him, bringing our hips together.

"Need you, alpha," I whine. I grind against his hard erection and do my best to try to lodge his cock where I burn.

Rif's fingers slide into my hair and he kisses me. *Devours* me with his tongue, lips, teeth. His fangs prick my lips, and I shiver when a hint of copper floods my mouth. I try to work him into me, but he's too strong. He keeps us locked belly to belly as he plunders my mouth.

"You're burning up," he says and wipes a drop of sweat from my brow. "You have to drink before I take you."

I shake my head. I don't want to drink. I want him locked inside me, but Jet reaches over Rif and places a cup to my lips. "Do as your alpha orders. Drink."

I take a sip. The cool water is a blessing. I greedily empty the cup, and it helps clear my mind. The fog that fills my skull lifts and I'm able to think. Rif's cock nudges my stomach. I sweep my finger over the soft mushroom head. The muscles of his stomach clench and he flinches. My gaze shoots to his and I let go of him.

His hand closes around mine. He squeezes my fingers around his girth. "Touch me all you like, om—" He swallows. "I like your hand on me. I want you to touch me. I'm merely sensitive. Explore all you like."

I swallow hard as my gaze drops back. "Are you sure?"

"I'm more than sure." His chuckle booms from his chest, its warmth making my mind grow fuzzy again. My hand drifts down to the ring at the base of his cock.

Rif groans. "Feels so good."

I trace the skin and it begins to thicken. His knot. The piece of him that will lock me to him. I'm sure that's what locked Stef inside me before I blacked out. That's not entirely true; I *blissed* out. That's the only description I can come up with to describe the space I soared into. I was aware, but there was no worry. No pain. Just perfection where there was nothing but ultimate fulfillment and contentment.

And yet, still there is something missing. A thrum deep inside me that shouldn't be there after sharing this intimacy.

"My knot is yours. I'll lock you to me, and I'll fill you with my seed and give you everything you need," he rasps.

Yes. That's exactly what I want. What I need. I'm not afraid of their knots. I yearn for them. The simmering heat blows into a furnace. My pussy flutters around nothing. I'm so empty. I tighten my grip around his erection, earning a grunt.

"Please, Rif. Give me your knot," I say.

He lifts me and rolls onto his back. My thighs part over his hips. Slick drips onto his abdomen with the anticipation of his shaft sliding inside me. I want to let him into me, to let him dissolve into my being, to take away the emptiness. His cock throbs, but he holds me above him. I try to wrangle down, but he doesn't let me move. In frustration I dig my nails into his chest, and my gaze flies to his face. I throb with pain. I need to be touched, caressed, and soothed.

"I'll give you everything, Adele. Always."

My heart almost stops, then restarts with a massive thud. He called me. By. My name. Joy fills me as he continues.

"This is the start of your new life. Here, with us. I won't stop you from leaving if you still want to go back to your planet, but I'll show you what you'll miss if you do," he says.

I half understand his words. Pain cramps my belly and I'm consumed with need, and all I can think of is that his cock needs to be inside me. A whimper breaks from my lips. His chest rumbles to life. His purr wraps around me like silk before it breaks off again. I told him not to purr for me, but I'm not the same female I was then. The creature I've changed into needs that sound like she needs oxygen. "Please. Keep going."

I relax, even though my tender pussy still pulses around nothing. Jet's hand glides along my side to cup my breast with his big palm and tweak my nipple.

"Tell me you understand," Rif says.

Stef parts my folds and drags his fingers through my wet, needy seam. Heat coils and tightens my belly. My head falls back, and my eyes slide shut as they pet and caress me.

"Use your words, omega, or Rif won't give you his cock," Jet says.

Their touch helps to relieve the driving ache. I need them as much as they need me. I can pretend I can leave them after this, but I can't hide from myself. Or my deepest desires.

"There's no need to be afraid," Stef whispers.

Those words stop me. The shock jolts something in me. Realizations I've hidden from come rushing back. Those realizations didn't go away because I ignored them. They hung on in my periphery, ready to snap back. And snap they do. They rock into me and shake me to my core.

No one cares for me on Earth. They use me for my work, and when there is no more funding, they'll send me away, despite the advances

I've made. I've loved no one since my father died. I've been too scared to let anyone close. It's meant I've lived in a state of fear for years.

Fear for my research.

Fear of cancer. Fear of death.

Fear to live.

Fear to love.

Until an unknown force thrust me into the lives of these alien alphas on another planet. It's a complete disruption to my life, but if it never happened, I'd still be wasting my life behind a microscope instead of living.

I'm not completely empty inside. Cords of their emotions weave through mine, seeking to join with me in a way that wouldn't be possible if I were still only human. I feel their vulnerability as they wait for my decision. They weren't lying when they said everything is up to me. These huge males, the most alpha of their species, are gentle enough to abide by my wishes. They're as lonely as I am. They understand my emptiness. The yearning to truly belong and be accepted.

"You called me Adele," I say to Rif.

His thumbs circle my hips, sending sparks shooting through me. "Because you asked me to."

I stare at him, then at Stef and Jet. There's hunger on their faces, but they're open too. They're letting me inside, asking me to give them myself and accepting everything about me.

"You hear me," I whisper.

"Always," Rif says.

The understanding binds me to them. Their cords tighten and burrow into my soul, where I welcome them. The creature I've become rises, letting me know exactly what I need to do.

I lean forward and bring my lips to Rif's neck, breathe in his scent, and lick a path on his skin, marking the place I'll leave my claiming bite.

"Claim me, alpha," I whisper, before I sink my teeth into his skin.

Chapter Seventeen

Adele

I'm an omega. I understand what that means now. I'm not weak. I don't exist to be used. I'm as powerful as the massive males surrounding me, but in a different way. I'm more *me* than I've ever been. I want these alphas—*my* alphas—with every part of my being. I surrender to the need that's greater than myself. I let it flow through me and embrace it.

My new nature rears through me as my mouth fills with Rif's blood. His hands tense before he roars his triumph. He rams me onto his cock and fills me until the tip kisses the top of my womb before he bites through the tender flesh on my neck.

"Take me. Make me yours. Give me your knot," I say. *Give me everything.*

Electricity skates over his skin. Bright red, it jumps from him to me. As his fangs pop through my skin, the electricity penetrates me. Momentary pain sears me before my shoulder grows numb and pure bliss races through me.

An awareness unfurls inside me, and Rif's emotions pour into me. The intense rush pools and absorbs as he finds a space and settles. I'm no longer alone. He's in me everywhere, an awareness that goes both ways. His soul is bared to mine, and he feels me as intensely in return.

A purr rattles from Rif's chest. The glorious sound is drawn up from the depths of his core. It vibrates and thrums into my chest. My nipples pebble and my abdomen clenches around his shaft.

Home. This is truly what home feels like.

"Mine." Rif eases his fangs from my neck and kisses me. His teeth catch on my bottom lip and heat spears through my belly. I rock on his cock, grinding down to embed the hard flesh as deep as possible. Liquid lust curls up my spine, driven higher by his answering desire.

"What . . . was that?" I gasp.

"It's the aitisal alruwh. Our soul connection. It only happens between mates destined for each other. See how special you are to us, omega? You're our completion," Rif rasps.

He plunders my mouth, squeezes my nape, and rolls his hips. Tension builds up, pleasure fluttering from my core. His shaft pulses around my clenched muscles. His hands slide to my hips. He draws me up and down, helping me gain the leverage I need. A low keening sound falls from me as his intense movements quicken.

His shaft grows bigger and waves of pleasure crash through me. His chest works like bellows as he uses me to thrust. I hold on to his chest, the only leverage I have. He bares his teeth and I see my blood around his fangs as he works me harder and faster until his fingers tense on my hips and he groans. Pleasure streaks through me, pulsing golden waves rushing through my body.

He grinds me to his hips as something inside me grows impossibly large. His knot expands and draws out my bliss. My climax shatters. Bursts of light break behind my eyes. I clamp my legs around his waist and drain him as he pumps rope after rope of cum into me.

My muscles quiver and I fall onto his chest. Rif wraps his arms around me, and his heart pounds under my ear as he holds me tight.

"My omega. My heart," he says as he presses a kiss to my temple.

I kiss his chest, unable to lift my head. "My alpha," I offer back.

I feel him inside me. His presence fills my chest. He's everywhere, but I'm not scared. Carrying a piece of him brings me peace. Comfort. Joy.

His fingers trail through my hair, and Stef and Jet smooth their fingers over my back. I'm reminded I have two more of my alphas to claim. My heart flutters and a thrill races through me.

"Our omega wants you," Rif says to them.

A smile tugs Jet's lips and his eyes blaze with desire. "I love seeing you sated and cared for. I, for one, will always want you in return."

He kisses me, with Rif still locked inside me. It still feels right to do this, to share myself in this way. We're a unit, a family. One omega to three alphas, as is right. My core tenses and Rif groans. "If you keep doing that, you'll be locked on me forever."

I lift my head and smile at him. "That sounds all right to me."

Rif brushes my sweaty, tangled hair from my forehead. "I love seeing you smile. It lights up your entire face, and I can see your soul dance in your eyes."

I blink at him, not realizing how he could use words like that. Amusement sparks where our souls join, and I laugh. The sound is light and giddy, and I know I haven't laughed like this in a long time.

"Will all our souls connect?" I ask.

"We're a bonded pack. You're our omega. Always. I can't wait to feel you inside me. To have you in my heart forever," Jet says.

The joy remains, but arousal rises beside it. Rif slips out of me and I still pulse with desire. The same unnamed need climbs within me, and I know exactly what I burn to do. "I want to claim you next, Jet."

He grips my hair as Rif rolls me off his torso to lie on my back in the bed. Jet kisses me again. This isn't a light kiss. This is a claiming kiss that uses his tongue, teeth, and fangs. "Always mine," he whispers.

He glides his hands up my leg and falls between my parted thighs. I wrap my legs around his waist and angle my hips. The tip of his cock nudges my core, and he slides in.

"Who do you belong to, Adele?" he says.

"You," I say immediately.

Satisfaction dances in his eyes as he begins to thrust. "I'm going to knot you. Claim you. Make you mine," he growls.

He pulls out of my channel and slams back inside me. Each pounding thrust pushes me into the bed. Bliss spirals as a coil tenses inside me.

"Yes, yes, yes," I chant as the special tension coils even harder. "Claim me, Jet. Please!"

I cry out and a tremor runs through my thighs as my orgasm spirals through me. Jet roars and pushes his knot inside me, filling me to perfection. Electricity bursts over his skin and crackles into me. His cock pulses and heat explodes in me as he releases. His fangs clamp on the other side of my neck. I don't notice the pain as it's soon replaced by sheer euphoria.

I don't think. I bite down on his shoulder as hard as I can. His blood pulses into my mouth and his essence lights up inside me. Joy, awe, pride. Those are the emotions that bloom in me as his arms band around me. He holds me in place with his cock, his teeth, his arms. His very essence. I hear the sound of my own heartbeat, my harsh breaths, the pulse behind my ears. I've never felt as close to anyone as my mates. Never felt so at peace.

And yet, there is one more place that needs to be filled.

I reach out to Stef as he lies on my other side. Heat, euphoria, and fatigue rise within me, but I will them away. I need to claim my last mate before I am complete. Jet's knot loosens and he pulls out of me.

"Next time I'll knot you all night long, but Stef needs you as much as you need him," Jet says.

Slick and cum pour from me, soaking my thighs and the sheets, but I don't care. I want our combined scents in my nest. I want to smear myself in them so that I'll wear these scents like clothing. The mating bond runs through Rif and Jet, gentle, fierce, and possessive. I want Stef's essence in me alongside theirs. Only then will I feel fully complete.

I cup his cheek and he tilts his head into my palm. His eyes close for a moment in rapture before they blink back open and I'm under his intense focus. "I'll be gentle, omega," he says.

"Want to claim you, Stef," I whisper.

"Want to claim you back, Adele," he says.

A cloud of heat washes through me, and my clarity of mind slips away. My body burns as my base need rises again. I want to claim Stef while I'm still cognizant. I want this to be the decision I make with full clarity of mind. Both of us deserve that.

"Let us help," Rif says.

They pick me up and turn me around so my cheek rests on the softest pillow. Stef moves behind me and lifts my hips. My thighs part to let him center himself behind me. My mouth waters. His cedar scent envelops me and bleeds into my veins. He leans over me, kissing a path down my spine, irreverent.

"Going to claim you, Adele. Going to sink my cock and my fangs into you and make you ours," he rasps.

My core clenches. Even though they've all been inside me, it still isn't enough. Not just yet. "Yes," I whisper.

His cock slides along the wet mess in my slit, coating himself in our combined juices. The hard rod of his arousal glides between my legs. I jerk when it hits my overly sensitive clit. My sex puckers with the need for my last mate to claim me.

I reach down my torso and fill my palm with rigid length. He shudders and I feel his thighs clench around me at my touch. I'm awed knowing I have this effect on him. That one touch can make him shudder like this. His cock throbs in my hand and the heat sears my palm.

Heat shimmers at the edges of my consciousness. I intrinsically know I don't have much time until it will steal me away. "Please, alpha. I need you."

"Love you, omega," Stef says as he lines himself up at my entrance.

Every part of my skin comes alive as he inserts himself and glides in. A cloud of heat comes off him as he fills me. My pulse ratchets up and my belly quivers.

"Please, please, please," I chant.

My body turns liquid as one hand folds over my hip and the other presses between my shoulder blades. I balance on my knees as my upper half rests on the bed and he slides in and out of me.

My eyes roll and my eyelids drift shut as my whole being focuses on that slick glide of his cock in and out of my channel. Every part of my body ignites. My cheek rocks against the pillow, and I can't stop the whine from passing out of me.

"So beautiful. So responsive." Stef's hand on my back glides down my spine to hold my other hip.

My core throbs and slick dribbles down my thighs. Stef's balls slap into my legs with every thrust. White pleasure sweeps over me, and the waves build with each pound. Crackles of electricity jump over his body and tickle mine. I can barely wait to feel his soul inside me. I dig my fingernails into the sheet and clench my eyes as pleasure coils tight in my belly.

I feel behind me for his arm, thread our fingers together, and draw his forearm to my mouth. I clamp down on him, biting through his flesh. My body shudders as he slams into me. His thrusts become rough and unhinged. My spine arches and my core clenches around his shaft as starlight bursts behind my eyes and his blood fills my mouth.

A low groan rips from him. He crashes against my thighs and pushes his throbbing shaft inside me, sinking as deep as he can. His knot expands behind my pelvic bone and locks me to him. Heat explodes inside me. Electricity spears through my back. My climax erupts through my body as I shatter into a million pieces.

He swoops down to bite the back of my neck. His fangs sink into me and I scream as another orgasm rockets through me. The pieces of me reassemble and weave his soul into mine.

Stef purrs. The sound sweeps into me, pours through me, heating me, enveloping me in everything that is them. Jet's purr joins Rif's and Stef's, and together they create a harmony that resonates inside and outside.

The space in my heart fills with prisms of light. Their essences resonate with strength and possession and something else much more hardy. Love. So. Much. Love. The intense kind that promises they'll always be at my side. They'll always see me. Hear me. Understand me. And I love them back just as fiercely. They are much more than alpha demon aliens. They're my mates. Trusted. Beloved. Adored.

I'm beyond sated. I'm . . . complete. Made whole. Their purrs sink into my blood, soothing and comforting me. And also arousing me. Liquid lust explodes along my nerve endings and bursts from my core. I sink into my most basic instinct and there's nothing to hold me back. My mind is a base haze of sexual need. My mates offer their cocks to me, pumping me full of their cum, caving to the demands of my body and my heat.

Time takes on no meaning as I cry for them. Plead for their cocks and their seed. I have no sentience other than the urges and needs rocketing through me. Bursts of their love carry me further into complete mindlessness.

Lucidity comes to me in odd brackets of time. I find myself waking in their arms, my body burning with intense arousal. Rif makes love to me while I feast on Stef's cock. Jet takes me on my hands and knees while I scream through an intense orgasm. They bathe me in the healing waters, hand-feeding me pieces of food I'll accept before I grow needy and demand they fill the deep ache in my core.

More. More, I want more. And they give it to me.

Until finally I wake, tired but fully aware. I have a full soul and a sated body. My mind is quiet. I'm surrounded by my alphas. My pack. This is the perfect end to a life I'd never let myself dream of.

Rif lifts his head, his dark eyes immediately falling on me and tracking over my body to make sure I'm all right. When he sees me watching him, his lips curl into a soft smile. "Adele, you're awake. Your heat's over."

I thread my fingers through his, feeling their souls tethered to mine. "Call me omega."

Chapter Eighteen

Omega

In D'Kali's lab, I sit and consider the technology that is both familiar and unfamiliar at the same time. It's so clean that it's hard to imagine how it was splattered with blood. Sometimes I glance at the floor and expect to see unmoving Ulgix bodies torn apart by my mates, but the white tiles sparkle and deny that such a battle even occurred. The Amadonians pulling apart the filter tanks outside the lab will always remember, though.

The largest Amadonian of them all strides into the lab and sees me looking out of the window. Rif immediately comes to me, drawn as though we're both at the end of a string that can only go so far for so long. He steps between my thighs and gets into my space. He tips back my head with no resistance from me and bends to collect my lips in a searing kiss. I'm swept away as I always am whenever any of my alphas kiss me, which is often. I squirm when my core pulses. My seam pools with a trickle of slick, and sweet apple blossom plumes around us.

"You need to kiss me again? It's only been an hour since the last time," I tease.

Rif smirks, and his black eyes gleam. "An hour is far too long for our omega to wait for attention."

"She hasn't waited an hour. I kissed her a few minutes ago," Stef says. His arms band around my shoulders when he stands behind me. He ducks his head and trails my temple with his lips. "Perhaps I should remind you what a proper kiss is, if you've forgotten."

"Stand aside while I show you how to really kiss an omega if her memory is failing her." Jet shoves Rif aside and makes a kissy mouth at me. "You two are amateurs compared to me."

I giggle and plant my palm on his chest to push him back, but he doesn't move. All of them are so tall and muscular I'd never be able to move any of them if they didn't allow it. "I'm not kissing any of you for at least another half hour. I have blood work to analyze."

I hop off the stool I'm sitting on, shove through Rif and Jet, and open up the hologram. A bright and colorful representation hovers in mid-air. I'm amazed at the Ulgix technology. If I'd had something like this on Earth, it would have made my research so much easier. I ignore the usual pang whenever I think of the life I left behind, even though the change was forced on me. I'm a better version of myself here. Happy with my mates. I wouldn't change where I am now. I have so much more than I ever thought I'd have. I was ready to wilt away for the sake of humanity, giving my life for others to live theirs.

"You've come a long way to understand the Ulgix technology," Stef says.

I tap the side of my head. "It took me a few days, but after I upgraded verbal and written language into the chip D'Kali put into my head, it was easier. It might take me a few years to get to the end of everything, but I can work out enough for now."

I spin the hologram of my blood cells. "No more mercury in my system." There are changes in my DNA structure too. I have the same molecules, but they're in a slightly different sequence.

If I thought I wasn't human anymore, the proof is irrefutable. The only question is, why was I taken from Earth and changed at all? For days the question has spun through my mind and an answer hasn't been forthcoming. Everything in science has a reason for existing. It's a matter of finding the reason. Unfortunately, when I don't know what I'm looking for, it makes the search for *Where's Waldo* increase from the size of a book to the size of a small city.

At least some of the changes are easy to make. Mercury could be stopped from going into the water system immediately. I'd told Rif what mercury was doing to his people. All my mates were outraged, but underneath I saw their confusion and hurt. They had trusted D'Kali and the Ulgix and thought they were saviors of their planet. D'Kali was their advisor for centuries. It blew my mind to understand how some species were so long-lived.

Rif ordered Lodin to stop the water filtering immediately, and the mines have been abandoned for now. Already their people have begun to change. They are healthier and less sickly. However, some of the betas who've mined for years are still affected. My exposure was only slight and, as I expected without continued exposure, the mercury naturally drained from my system.

"I'm working on a chelator you'll be able to give the miners this afternoon," I say. "It'll work as an agent to help get the mercury out of their systems."

I flick the hologram to show how blood cells move through veins. "See here? This is where the cells picked up mercury." I change the hologram to represent the cells in a diagram format. "See how it changed the chemical composition? In the alphas, there was another protein added. This technology is amazing. It can show the transition of cells before taking the blood. I can go back months if I want to. If I had this technology back on Earth, it would have made my job so much easier. Testing can take so long. Long enough for people to forget you're doing it, and . . ." I've forgotten myself. I turn to the alphas and ready myself for closed-off expressions of boredom. "I'm sorry. Sometimes I forget how boring this is to others."

"This isn't boring. Not when we see you come alive. I love seeing you so excited. I think you're truly amazing, Adele." Rif strokes his knuckles along my jawline, and my breath catches at the possessive pride in his eyes. "We'd be fools if we didn't find joy in the same things you do."

I feel my cheeks heat and know my face is going bright red. "Love it when your skin changes color like this," Jet says, a smirk forming on his lips. "It reminds me of when I'm feasting on your flesh and you change to this beautiful color beneath my mouth and tongue."

The heat that is never far away begins to simmer. As much as I want to make love to them, they could waylay me for the rest of the day, and there are a few things I want to do first. I clear my throat. "The alphas at the funeral service who went into rut after they . . ." My cheeks burn anew. I still haven't quite come to terms with the scent I release. The sweet, sugary scent that can send alphas into rut is a known omega trait and something I will study.

"Look, brothers. Her cheeks are bright red. She almost matches the color of our skin," Stef says.

"I wonder if she's changing color all over her body. Although, I do like her pale tone. It contrasts so deliciously with ours when she's naked and writhing in pleasure between us," Jet says.

I push on, determined to ignore the arousal that grows more urgent. My scent perfumes around me, my arousal no longer a secret from my alphas. "Their blood shows traces of enormous amounts of testosterone. I can only think that their adrenal glands were agitated and whatever caused the agitation has now gone. They're nowhere near as aggressive as before," I say.

Rif lifts the hair at the back of my neck and blows on the perspiration building there. The shiver steals through my whole body. "So hot, omega." My eyelids fall closed for a moment as he licks my skin. "Mmm. Delicious."

I gather myself, something that is becoming increasingly hard to do. I force myself to step away and move to the controls, compelling my legs to move away from them. They are stiff, my knees locking, as I shuffle the two steps from Rif's addictive leather scent. I want my feet to take me back to him so I can bury my nose in his neck and open my thighs so he can brush his cock against my aching pussy.

I grip the side of the bench and Rif chuckles. "Do what you need to do, Adele. I can see you fighting. We'll tend to you when you're ready. There's no urgency."

"Says you," I say.

That is a true and false statement. There is some urgency because my omega nature is fast overcoming my logical mind, and I know where that will take me. *Nest*. I look around the bare lab and the too-hard and cold floor. Not good enough. When I make love to my alphas, it will be in a comfortable, warm, safe nest piled high with soft furs and blankets, where I'll lose myself in my alphas' attentions and seek the pleasure my body was made for.

Focus!

"The Ulgix blood shows they're an entirely different species." I speak a little too loudly. I find the button that will display the blood cells taken from the dead D'Kali and press a little too hard. A hologram appears, but shows a different angle from the one I've previously studied. I focus on a nucleotide I'd never seen before.

"What's . . . that?" I mutter.

My alphas surround me. Their scents tease my nostrils, but the ice in my veins keeps me focused. I spin the hologram and enlarge a part that is a true *Where's Waldo*. "I would never have looked for this because I never knew it existed."

"What is it, Adele?" Jet says.

I hear him, but I'm deep in my thought process. I've been known to lose hours and days when I get like this. I'm a victim to it as much as my new biology, but the alphas stand back and let me work and do what I need to do. They support me. Fully and completely.

"This can't be, but . . ." I can't ignore the evidence. "Let me just . . ." I turn the hologram and run a sequence that shows the development of the tiny nucleotide. "It has a nitrogenous base, but it can't be attached the way it has. It's impossible, but . . ."

My blood turns to ice as I watch the development of this particular atom devolve through time until it's not there. The only way something like that has developed is if it has been spliced there intentionally.

"When did the Ulgix land on this planet?" I say.

"They've been here for six hundred of our years," Rif says. A deep line has formed between his brows.

I point at the place on the DNA strand before the nucleotide has grown. "See this?" They nod and I fast forward. "See that?"

Rif's brows lower over his pitch-black eyes and he nods. Stef and Jet stand shoulder to shoulder and peer at the small node.

"The Ulgix have genetically engineered themselves. The timeline is six hundred years." I begin to pace, my mind racing. "It's impossible, but the evidence is right in front of my eyes. There can be no other logical explanation."

"Tell us what this means," Stef says. He shifts on his feet. I go to him and wrap my arms around him because I've made him uncomfortable, and I need the safety of his arms as well.

"It means the Ulgix are a species that thrives on mercury. Unlike most species, such as you and me, mercury will poison and kill, but mercury works in the opposite way for the Ulgix. Instead of killing them, it *extends* their life.

"No wonder they came here. Your planet is rich in mercury. They basically found the fountain of youth on your planet. With the mercury here, they could genetically engineer themselves to live forever..."

The sequencing on the hologram changes again. The time depicting D'Kali's DNA going further back than six hundred years. I pull from Stef's arms and watch as the years fly backward. My eyes blur and I stagger when the final date appears.

"That can't be right." I move to the controls to make sure the information is correct, and run the same test three different times with the same result. I press my shaking fingers to my mouth.

I look up at my alphas—powerful males who protect everyone around them. It would have been impossible for them to understand what the Ulgix were doing to them. "Tell me why the Ulgix came to your planet."

"Our population was dying. They came to help us find a cure for The Death and helped win the Solice war," Jet says.

"The Death is another way to say mercury poisoning." I remember what Rif had told me about the beginning of the end to their society. The steady downward spiral of a great race of people to fracture them apart. The Ulgix could rule through division. War is constructive. Secrets can be hidden. They purposefully bred out an entire subspecies of alphas and omegas vital to this race. I pace the lab, sweat building under my arms, my heart picking up its pace as the pieces click together and a horrific picture begins to form.

"This was all planned. I think they started to poison your people before they came here. I think they set it up to arrive at a time when you needed help. I bet it was convenient, them coming here to 'help,' when all along they were killing you. They helped in your war to build false trust. Poisoning you and taking your planet's natural resources to use for their own purposes. They began to breed out your alphas and omegas so they could control the remaining population of betas to mine your mercury. Your landscape is perfectly built for it. The volcanic activity. The coal that contains a stupidly high percentage of easily mined mercury. Earth has the same pockets of activity. They throw back your society to pre-technology times so there's no way you can find any of this out, making your lives about survival instead of progression. It's not even that brilliant a plan. There's plenty of times society on Earth has fallen in the same way . . ."

I stop pacing and whirl to face my alphas as a dark pit opens inside me. They begin to purr in their need to comfort me as my emotions pool on their side of our bond. The picture in my mind has gone from simply horrific to terrifying. I'd take horrifying at this stage, but I know I'm not wrong.

My ability to make connections is one of the reasons why I was funded for my research. I wish I wasn't blessed with this intelligence and that it wasn't working like the biological super-computer it is. In this moment, I wish I was anything else, but the evidence is clear.

My gaze slides past my alphas to the clean and shining spacecraft in the distance. At the rows and rows of them deep within the cavern. A whole army of them, ready to take flight. Ready to start the same slow invasion and annihilation of another species. A species very similar in DNA sequencing to that of the Amadonians. A species they can change as easily as they have already done with technology that rivals magic.

I'm not here by chance. I'm the first step in a scientific experiment. I'm the hypothesis and the research. I'm here as a result of very careful planning.

A scuffle steals my attention, and Lodin bolts into the room. His eyes are wild and his clothing is disheveled, and the fur he wears over his shoulders is strung around his neck. He skids on the polished tiles in his haste, panting heavily. Sweat beads his brow as he fights to contain himself. I know what he's going to say before he has a chance to utter a sound.

I push past the wall of muscle as my alphas stand in front of me, no doubt to protect me from Lodin's sudden appearance. "More human females have been found, haven't they?"

Lodin blinks, his face slack before he pulls himself together. He gives me a fast nod and swallows. "Our spies have returned. They say the Innis Tile alpha warlords have a captive. Another human female appeared from nowhere, much like you. They took her, and she hasn't been seen since."

I rear back. My alphas close around me, soothing me with their purrs, their touches, and the deep calm they send through our bond. My heart still pounds because there is another female! Another woman, alone and confused like me, has been stolen from Earth. I turn to my alphas. "I need to get to her. Find her. Help her."

I was fortunate they found me, but this other woman might not be so lucky. She could be harmed. Hurt. There's no telling the state she could be in. "Where is this Innis Tile? We have to go there and get her out."

Rif's hand is heavy on my shoulder. A weight of a different kind winds through me. I put my hand over my belly, but the darkness persists. Apprehension. Disquiet. Trepidation. They grow barbs as they churn in my stomach.

Rif's deep voice rumbles in my ear. "The Innis Tile is our neighboring kingdom, the land of ice and frost, and we've been at war with them for over four hundred years. We'll find your human female, omega, but it won't be easy."

I wasn't the only Ulgix experiment.

There's no telling how many others D'Kali or other Ulgix might have stolen.

Even now some of them could be on their way to Earth to start the systematic poisoning and invasion of another world. Who knows how many worlds they've already done this to, but I have their technology and I'll make it my mission to find out.

***

I hope you loved this steamy, omegaverse goodness. You won't stay sated for long. **Stolen by the Barbarian Warlord** is the second in the **Stolen Planet** series.

***

One minute I'm seducing the corrupt politician bribing my sister and the next I'm thrown onto an ice-packed mountain.

Giants with ice-blue skin, shoulders for days, thick thighs and huge...packages, rescue me from certain death. They say I'm theirs to do with as they please. To pleasure. To claim. To breed.

When I'm in – heat – I won't stand a chance because I'm not human anymore. I'm something else. A rare omega according to them. Their...mate.

I don't have time for this. I need to get home and save my sister.

She's the one female who will complete our pack, but she rejects her nature.

Our omega wants to go back to her planet, but soon enough she'll see her true home is with us. We'll do everything within our power to bring on her heat no matter how much she protests.

She says she doesn't know what an omega is, but she will submit.

She is ours.

***

Chapter One

Sarah

It's taken three whiskey-and-cokes and two hours of sickening flirting, but Williams finally goes to empty his bladder. I slot the USB with the hacking software into his personal computer and let my eyes stray to the closed door of his office's private bathroom.

I hear him humming to himself above the sound of urination, and I barely stop from retching. I'm down to my camisole and skirt, and I wasn't sure what excuse I could come up with to stop his skin-crawling advances. If he believes I'm even halfway attracted to him, I can only boil it down to his ego. Plain and simple.

The guy is in his mid-fifties, balding, with a serious paunch. The one thing going for him is his power. If I were a greedy slime-bucket like the rest of the people on his dirty-laundry list, I wouldn't care about his sweaty palms and his smarmy smile. The only thing I want to do with him is find enough evidence to make his inevitable arrest irrefutable. Once I have what I need to nail him, I'll take it to the right people—those who aren't on his payroll.

Unfortunately, that's a long list and includes my boss who fired me today because I pushed this story when he told me to drop it. Multiple times. I chalk up Andrew Scott's name onto the growing list of people Michael Williams has paid off.

I'd wondered why my articles about the victims of Williams' crimes never got published, replaced instead by glowing stories of how much the councilman was doing for his community. When I confronted my boss and editor, I found out why with a finger pointed at the door and a warning to drop things if I was smart. I'm not that type of girl; I mean, I'm smart, just not easily bought. I've worked too hard and for too long to let scumbags like Michael Williams get off free.

Not after what he's done to his latest victim, who happens to be my sister. He doesn't know we're related, which is sad because Emily has worked as his personal assistant for the past six months and he hasn't noticed our similarities. Our raven-black hair and bright blue eyes are startling enough to connect us as Johnson sisters.

Emily loved her job for the first two months, then she came across anomalies in payments made from public funds to private accounts. Large amounts that didn't add up. She questioned Williams about it because she's damn good at her job. He didn't deny it, but he threatened her husband and baby if she ever went to the cops, and that's when she came to me and we hatched this plan.

Four months later and we have some evidence, but I want the gold that'll lock him up in a five-inch-thick Perspex cell similar to the one in the television program The Blacklist. The idiot kept Emily on as his PA, thinking he had her under his thumb. Of course, she hated it, but it enabled her to keep a close eye on what he did and where he saved his incriminating files.

It's all on this laptop. She left it on the cabinet beneath a stack of files in his office instead of the locked drawer he gets her to put it into. It's why I'm here, trying to get him drunk enough that he needs to take a piss so I can get to it. Unfortunately he has a cast-iron bladder for a man well into his fifties, and I've been forced to keep my lunch in my stomach while I try to look interested in him.

I watch the solid blue bar creep up the screen as though I can will it to go faster. A bright red flare reflects off the computer screen from outside the window. It's the sun flare they've been warning us about, but then I let it go. I have more important things happening than a solar flare. Eighty percent. Ninety. Almost there. The toilet flushes and water flows from the faucet.

Copy faster, you fucker.

Static runs across the computer screen. It rises like mist on a winter's night, then invades the room, swirling around me. I reel backward, shock stealing my breath. No! No, no, no, no, no. What's happening? I tap the side of the computer, but my hand passes through the device.

Am I hallucinating? I can't move. I can't blink. My stomach rolls around thick sludge.

Williams' office disappears, and I'm surrounded by streaks of starlight. The darkness of the universe yawns around me. I can't feel my body. I'm as insubstantial as the light streaming around me. Or maybe I'm racing through it. It's hard to tell what I am or where I exist.

A tunnel twists around me, shooting me through it, curving one way then the next. Whatever I'm made of comes undone. I shatter apart and in the blink of a moment, I either exist only in this vacuum or not at all. I'm nothing and everything all at once before I come back together again, but not quite in the same way. I can't pinpoint what's different in me, but it's there, like a switch that's been off all my life has been turned on in a way I never thought possible.

I'm not hurtling through the tunnel now. I'm falling. Tumbling through air. Gravity catches my body. Freezing wind cuts through my clothing. My vision is whitewashed, and I'm thrown into a blanket of snow.

This isn't the powderpuff snow depicted in cartoons and rom-com movies set in a ski resort. This snow is made from icy shards that sting and bite. I roll, out of control, across the hard-packed ice until I thankfully come to a stop.

I try to untangle my limbs, but it's hard to move. The frigid air cuts into me, freezing my bones and turning my blood to sleet. I have to sit up. Have to move. I know I'll freeze to death if I don't. But I can't. My muscles are heavy, and I've been churned up from the inside out.

My work skirt and silk camisole are useless. They're drenched and freezing against my skin. I might as well be naked. My teeth chatter so hard I might chip a tooth, and I shiver so violently all I can do is draw my ineffective mess of limbs into a ball and wait until my body freezes solid. It won't take long in this weather, this ice. Snowflakes rain down on me and melt on my skin.

How am I here?

Did I just die?

Where the fuck am I?

An inhuman bellow shreds the air. It's a cross between a lion's roar and a wolf's howl. The hairs on my arms rise. I've lost a shoe, but that's the least of my concerns. Something heavy crunches on the ice and comes toward me. I clamber onto haunches, fingers digging into the snow. A thick fog hangs around me. Snowflakes pelt me, and a chill air rustles the few trees surrounding me.

A branch snaps and echoes behind me. I whirl around. I don't know, but I'm too scared to worry about bodily functions when I'm looking into the maw of certain death. A creature stalks toward me, so white it blends in with the mist and the piles of snow surrounding it.

I look up and up and up. Wide, round, pitch-black eyes stare intently at me. Its eyes are the only color on its face and body. A triangular nose sits above a massive muzzle that hangs open. Rows of serrated teeth drip thick yellow saliva onto the snow. It resembles a cat and I wish it was, but this animal is all predator.

It raises its nose, the nostrils flaring, before it lowers its head and slinks around a tree. Shaggy white fur hangs to the ground, covering the rest of its body. Wicked curved claws as long as my forearm spear the snow. I'm definitely the prey.

I leap up and try to make a run for it. My feet have gone numb. I pump my legs as fast as I can, but my muscles resist movement. I fall forward and my face lands in the snow. I don't notice if I've hurt myself because blind panic whites my mind with the certainty that these are the last few seconds of my life. I whip around and onto my back as the creature leaps.

A blur of light blue and white scales flashes past me. A creature crashes into the beast, takes it to the ground, and stamps on it. I peer at the enormous body that has taken such a predator to the ground. It's a greater predator, the apex of beasts, and all I can do is stare at its shining scales, its unfurling leathery wings, and the long, pointed tail that thumps into the snow. It raises its head and bellows. Its electric blue eyes roll in its head, and it gnashes lethal white teeth at the animal underneath it. It snaps its wings, and the whip-crack resounds through the trees.

Dragon. The word slices through my panic. The new beast is a snow dragon that blends perfectly with the landscape.

The dragon turns its head toward me. Its nostrils round, making a snuffling sound as it sniffs. It might be cute if I didn't imagine myself being crunched between its teeth. It would only take one, maybe two bites before it would swallow me. The furry beast flips onto its back, twists away from the dragon, and dashes off into the mist. I've escaped one predator for another.

And holy hell, because another dragon rushes through the underbrush and comes up short when it sees me. This dragon's eyes are pale pink, and an iridescent pink sheen flashes through its scales. Its mane, made from strands of the same pale color, runs down its neck and waves in the breeze. They're beautiful. Unearthly. And predators who both have their sights set on me.

When figures jump from the backs of the dragons, I dig my heels into the snow and push back. I hadn't noticed them before, which says something about me because the way these males stalk toward me screams more apex predator. Larger than the giant cat and the dragons.

"I've died and gone to Middle-earth." The words slip out, but these are no hobbits.

They are not gentle. Or small. They prowl toward me on tree-trunk-sized legs. Broad shoulders sit above massive chests. Cloaks of white fur cover their shoulders. The fur is thick and plush and goes up to their ears. I might say that the fur bulks them out, but one glance at their huge, round biceps tells me it doesn't.

Thick thigh muscles push out their light-tan breeches, and heavy boots lace to their knees. Nothing can disguise the massive bulges between their thighs that let me know they are undeniably male.

"Awmygha," the one with long, black, silky hair rumbles. His voice is a growly boom that sinks into me and turns my abdomen to water.

I pull my gaze from the package he's sporting between his thighs to his stunning eyes that are so dark they could be almost black if I didn't catch the lighter flecks that reflect the snow. His nose is narrow and straight and set over plump lips that are made for kissing. His skin is as dark as his eyes. Dark navy on dark navy, as deep as the universal sky I flew through.

"Man hi wakayf 'atat litakun huna?" the other male asks. This male is the polar opposite of his companion. His close-cropped white hair frames a rounder face. Elven ears peek from the jagged strands and swivel in my direction. His eyes remind me of a summer sky, boundless and clear, peering at me with what seems to be the same awe as the other one.

His lips are a darker blue and flare wide as he openly regards me. A myriad of emotions passes across his face. Shock. Awe. Curiosity. And last of all, unmistakable heat.

The males stand over my prone form, their legs planted like solid trees in the snow. They steal my entire focus. I try to find a word for them. Goblins. Orcs. Elves. None suit, then my mind snaps: aliens.

Holy fucking whizz on a stick, these males are aliens!

Tantalizing scents drift toward me. Pine and frost—which remind me of my grandmother's farm—and fresh snow tinged with mint mingle in the air. My mouth waters. Hmmm. Delicious.

A wave of languid heat from nowhere rolls through me, contrasting with my frozen body. Something tightens in my abdomen. My core swells and wet heat dribbles between my legs. What the hell?

Have I somehow hurtled through space and turned inside out? My feet and hands are so frozen I can't feel them, I'm clearly losing my damned mind, and I've dampened my panties.

The dark male's nostrils flare as he drags air deep into his lungs. What's with all the sniffing? His skin lights up with a dazzling blue glow. His eyes spark from deep navy to electric blue.

The lighter male sucks in a fast breath. His shoulders jerk as he also glows with a streak of blue that originates from deep within him. His eyes glow so bright it lights his face and the surrounding snow.

The glow recedes and the dark male's skin returns to its navy hue. The snow puffs out as he falls to his knees and reaches toward me. "Hi rafiqatuna. La 'usadiq 'anana wajadnaha akhyran."

I flinch out of his reach even though the urge to lean into him feels like the most natural thing in the world, but I don't know him. I don't know where I am and I'm fucking terrified. "Don't touch me."

His fingers clench and slowly form a fist. It stays raised between us. "Ala taelam man nahnu? 'Ala tasheur bih Aydan?"

A line forms between the white brows of the lighter blue male, and he kneels next to me as well. "Nahn rifaquka. Lan nudhiaka."

"I don't know who you are or what you want with me, but I want to go home. There's something very important I have to do. My sister is relying on me and . . ." My throat closes and I can't speak. It might be shock. Or I'm becoming a block of ice. Or maybe because the only reason I can think to explain where I am and why very real, very large aliens are within touching distance is that somehow, someway, I've crossed the universe and am on another freaking planet.

How is that possible? And fucking why has it happened?

I take one great big gulp of air and try to keep everything in, but it's impossible. A sob bursts from me and I can't stop. My chest heaves. I'm so cold my teeth rattle in my head, and I shiver so violently I think I put my hips out.

Silver-hair cries out. He moves so fast I don't realize he's wrapping me up in his enormous fur cloak, settling me on his thick, hard thighs, and pressing me into the planes of his warm, broad chest. I struggle because he's an alien and I don't know why the hell I find him so attractive.

He arranges me on his lap as though I'm not doing my best to push off that massive chest and pulls me to him with no effort at all. It's so easy for him. His body mass is easily five times mine, and it's all well-honed muscle. His fingers clasp the back of my head and smoosh my face against his hot skin.

Fresh mint drifts around me, and I drag the scent into my lungs. I can't help it. I inhale as much as I can, savoring the flavor as it seeps into my bloodstream. His chest rumbles to life, and the most delicious sound reverberates through me. The fight drains from me as though I don't have a will. I want to curl up in his warmth instead. I'm . . . safe. Protected.

Which makes no sense at all.

An awareness unfurls, raising its head in my core as heat steals through me. My stomach cramps, and wetness gushes from me again. Sweet caramel blooms upward. A tremor works through silver-hair's hands before he strokes a massive palm over my back.

Another purr joins his as blue-eyes moves behind me. His massive hands fold over my shoulders, and I'm engulfed in heat and masculine attention. I can't think. I should be fighting. I need to get away. I have to . . . Their purrs intensify, and my bones turn to liquid.

"Awmygha. 'Ant lina." Blue-eyes nuzzles my hair.

I should be shaking, sobbing, running, but I'm not. I'm soft and compliant. They could do anything to me, and I'm helpless to stop them. I'm thoroughly trapped.

READ STOLEN BY THE BARBARIAN WARLORD TODAY...